never eighteen

MEGAN BOSTIC

Houghton Mifflin Harcourt

Boston   New York   2012

All rights reserved. Published in the United States by Graphia, an imprint of
Houghton Mifflin Harcourt Publishing Company.

For information about permission to reproduce selections from this book,
write to Permissions, Houghton Mifflin Harcourt Publishing Company,
215 Park Avenue South, New York, New York 10003.

Graphia and the Graphia logo are trademarks of
Houghton Mifflin Harcourt Publishing Company.

www.hmhbooks.com

The text of this book is set in Garamond.

Library of Congress Cataloging-in-Publication Data
Bostic, Megan.
Never eighteen / by Megan Bostic.
p. cm.
Summary: Seventeen-year-old Austin, aware that life is short, asks his best friend
and secret love, Kaylee, to take him to visit people and places in and around Tacoma,
Washington, so that he can try to make a difference in the time he has left.
ISBN 978-0-547-55076-3
[1. Conduct of life—Fiction. 2. Interpersonal relations—Fiction. 3. Sick—Fiction.
4. Cancer—Fiction. 5. Death—Fiction. 6. Tacoma (Wash.)—Fiction.] I. Title.
PZ7.B649555Nev 2012
[Fic]—dc22
2011001029

Manufactured in the United States of America
DOC 10 9 8 7 6 5 4 3 2 1

4500334943

Dedication

To my parents, who always believed in me,
even when I didn't believe in myself.
To Rusty, without whom this story
would not have been written.
And to my daughters, Mary and Rachel.
They are my light.

day one . . .

chapter one

I had the dream again. The one where I'm running. I don't know what from or where to, but I'm scared—terrified, really. I wake drenched in sweat. Jumping out of bed, I immediately head to my computer.

I need to get some things done this weekend, and I'm running out of time. God, I hope Kaylee can help. What if she asks what I'm doing? I can't tell her, can I? No. She'd try to stop me, I'm sure of it. Shit, I hope she doesn't have to work. I should have checked. Without her Mustang, I may not be able to do this, and I want to, I need to. Otherwise, things may just continue as they always have: painful, motionless. Like treading water. You stay afloat, but you never really get anywhere. A flash, a flicker of life, that's all I want. I don't think it's too much to ask.

I sit at the computer and stare at the monitor, wondering where to begin. I need to make a list. It's hard, but soon it all comes rushing to me—people, places, things. Over and over

I think of Kaylee. I want her to be there. Need her to be beside me through all of it.

I type until my thoughts die down, come to a stop. I hit Print, grab the list, and shove it into the pocket of my jacket, hanging on my closet door. I look in the mirror. I've changed so much in the last year, physically, emotionally, mentally. I may be smaller now, but my heart and mind are stronger.

These last few months I've come to realize that life doesn't wait. If we stand still it passes us by, and by the time we understand that, it may be too late. The people I see this weekend—I hope they're okay with this. I want them to take hold of it and not let go. I hope they at least listen. If they don't, it will kill me.

I grab a shoebox that's been sitting in my closet. It held the new pair of green Converse high-tops my mom bought me before the school year started. Cool shoes. I take the lid off the box and put it on my bed. I pack the box with books, CDs, pictures, my poetry notebook, things that are important to me. I won't have everything I need until Sunday night. On Monday, it goes to Kaylee's for safekeeping.

It's late, and I have a full weekend ahead of me. I put the lid back on the shoebox and place it on the top shelf of my closet. Out of sight. There's no need for my mom to find it. She wouldn't understand.

I shut off the light and climb back into bed. My body's tired, but my mind keeps working, churning. I'm anxious, nervous, thinking of what to say, what to do. Sleep comes with difficulty, but in the end, it still comes.

chapter two

"Where are you off to?" Mom pries, like moms do, as I head out the door, down the walk, past her. She's already outside on her knees, pulling weeds, needing to keep busy these days. It's cold out, but at least it's not raining like it usually does in the Pacific Northwest in September. It wouldn't matter anyway. She'd garden in the heat, the rain—hell, probably even the snow. Gardening is a sanctuary of sorts for her, her place to escape, her place to forget. She leans on her garden heavily these days, but I'm hoping to change that. It would be nice if she could just enjoy it again.

"Just going out for a while," I answer, still groggy. My body wanted to stay in bed longer, but my mind was ready to get the weekend started.

"Is that all you're eating for breakfast?" She eyeballs me suspiciously, nodding to the shiny red apple in my hand. I don't have much of an appetite these days, and on top of the anxiety I feel this morning, the apple seemed like the only thing I could handle.

"I'm not that hungry," I answer. She doesn't press, and her suspicious expression relaxes into one that I can describe only as love with a hint of sadness.

"When will you be home?"

"I'm not sure. Probably past dinner," I answer. I hope she doesn't grill me. Telling my mom my plans would be worse than telling Kaylee. She'd probably tell me I'm crazy, that I should mind my own business. In fact, she probably wouldn't let me out of the house. It's best to remain vague.

She stares into my eyes knowingly, smiles, and says, "Watch for cars."

I'm seventeen and my mom still tells me to watch for cars. I suppose she feels like her job is near ending, but that as long as I'm here and she's here, she has to look out for my safety and well-being. After what happened to Jake, I can't really blame her. It's true what they say: a mother's work is never done. As I continue down the walkway, then the sidewalk, I feel my mom's eyes on me until I'm well out of her sight.

chapter three

My first stop is Kaylee's house. She's been my best friend since third grade, since the day she started school at Skyline Elementary, the day I came to her rescue on the playground. It's also the day I fell in love with her.

She lives four blocks away. What would be an easy walk for most drains me. I ring the bell and wait. Her mom answers the door.

"Hi, Mrs. Davis. Is Kaylee here?"

"Austin, I don't know why you insist on calling me Mrs. Davis. I've already told you to call me Jen. Everyone calls me Jen. Even the girls call me Jen when they're mad at me." She laughs.

Two bad things happened in sixth grade. One of these things is the reason I can't bring myself to call her Jen. I have too much respect for her.

"Kaylee's still in bed, Austin," she says.

"Can I wake her?" I ask.

"If you dare."

I climb the stairs, then slowly and silently open the first door to the right, Kaylee's room. I sneak in quietly, not wanting to scare her; I sit down on the edge of her bed and stare. She's so beautiful lying there, her arms wrapped around the stuffed cat I gave her for her birthday that she so lovingly named Stinky Cat. There have been so many times I've wanted to tell her I love her but couldn't. If she didn't feel the same, it would have put this weird spin on our relationship, and I would rather have her like this, as a friend, than not at all. So, I keep quiet.

Wanting to remember her right here in this moment of beauty and sleep, I pull my Cyber-shot out of my pocket. A gift from my grandmother, my camera is my most prized possession. It goes everywhere with me. You never know when you might come across something funny, or strange, or moving, or even incredible, as Kaylee is to me right now. I snap the picture. I check the digital image before it disappears. Perfection, thank God, because no second chances, as the clicking wakes her. Her bright blue eyes open slowly, blink a few times, then rest on my face. She smiles up at me, a smile I could imagine only belonging to an angel.

"Yo, Kaylee. 'Sup," I say, a private joke between the two of us. We both love the movie *Superbad* and have watched it together at least a million times.

"Hey," she answers. It sends my pulse racing and my

spine prickling. She stretches her arms up over her head and lets out a massive yawn.

"Ew," I say. I fan my hand in front of my face, suggesting that her breath stinks. She punches me lightly in the arm.

"Are you working today?" I ask.

"No."

"So what are you going to do?"

"Whatever you're doing," she answers. My heart nearly leaps through my chest.

"Well, you better get up. We have a long day ahead of us."

"What's going on?"

"I have a million places to go. Can you drive me?"

"Sure. I'll be down in twenty," she says. She throws back her covers. I catch a glimpse of her pajamas, which are just gray UW sweat shorts and a white tank top, but still my pulse quickens again. I keep that image in my head as I go downstairs to wait.

"Hi, *Aaauuuustin,*" Jordanne, Kaylee's youngest sister, greets me. She always pronounces my name like that, as if she has a southern drawl.

"Hi, Jordanne. How are you today?"

"Good. Whatcha doin'?" she asks.

"Waiting for Kaylee," I answer.

"Why?"

"Because we're hanging out today."

"Do you love her?" The question catches me off-guard.

"We're friends. Friends love each other."

"I'm friends with Billy Fletcher, and I don't love him."

"Maybe you're too young," I say.

She ignores the answer, continues with the interrogation. "Are you going to marry her?"

"No." That I knew for sure.

"Why?"

"It's complicated," I answer, hoping that ends it.

"Well, will you marry me, then?"

I laugh. "Let me think about it. That's a serious commitment, you know." She shrugs and runs off, giggling.

Seconds later, Maddie, the middle sister, comes barreling down the stairs in her pajamas.

"Hi, Maddie," I say. When she looks up at me, her face flushes red, and then she turns around and runs back upstairs.

I hear her screaming, "Kaylee! Why didn't you tell me Austin was here? I'm in my pajamas! God, you're such an idiot!"

I can't help but laugh. I've seen Maddie in her PJs loads of times, but now that she's thirteen and has boobs, though small ones, she must feel a little more self-conscious about it.

I think both Jordanne and Maddie have crushes on me. If only their sister felt the same.

A few minutes later, Kaylee comes down the stairs, smiling, blond hair still wet from showering. She's wearing jeans and a blue sweater. She looks hot.

"Ready?" she asks.

"Ready."

"Where are you kids off to?" Mrs. Davis asks just as we're about to leave.

"Mom! Do you have to know everything?" Kaylee cries.

"It's okay," I say, touching her shoulder, then turn to her mom. "I have a few things I need to take care of this weekend. Things I've been meaning to do for a while now. I need Kaylee to drive me. We might be out kind of late. Is that okay?"

She stares me in the face with understanding, nods, and, without a word, heads back toward the kitchen.

chapter four

Kaylee's car, her prized possession, her baby, her red 1969 Ford Mustang. She bought that car with the money she made working at the café in the Lakewood Barnes and Noble, a job she applied for because of her addictions to coffee and books. *Pride and Prejudice* is her favorite. The car's not in mint condition by any stretch of the word—rust spots, torn leather interior, windshield wipers that only work on high— but it's hers. She owns it. She earned it.

More than once I've wondered if it would get us where we're going, be it Seattle, downtown, or just around the block. It hasn't failed us yet. I hope it won't today. I slide into the passenger seat, buckle my seat belt, and put my feet up on the dash, which Kaylee immediately slaps down.

"Get your feet off Candy. She doesn't like that," she says.

"Candy? Is that the name this week?" Kaylee has wanted to name her car since the day she bought it. All classic cars have names based on their personalities, she told me once. So far, this car has been Glory, China, Cherry, and Blaze. Now Candy.

"You should name it Apple," I say.

"Apple? Why Apple? That's stupid."

I pull the apple I brought from home out of my pocket, hold it up, toss it, turn it around. "Because she's red, shiny, smooth, and sweet."

"No, it's Candy. Plus, it's the same thing."

"Candy is not part of the four basic food groups," I say, chuckling, then take a huge bite.

"Sure it is. Candy, coffee, pizza, and gum, right?"

"You're such a dork," I say. She sticks her tongue out.

"You could have gotten your own driver's license, you know. Then I wouldn't have to chauffeur you around all the time."

"What's the point? Besides, I like it when you chauffeur me around."

"Whatever. Where are we going first?" she asks.

"Jake's house," I say, mouth full of apple.

"Jake's house?" she asks.

"Yep."

"Why?"

"I want to talk to his mom."

"Ooookaaaaaaay," she says as she starts the car.

I touch her arm. "Wait. Turn the car off." When she does I say, "If I tell you what I'm doing, do you promise to still drive me?"

"I guess so."

"There are some things I want to do, some crazy things, some wild things, some fun things, things I've never done, things I've never seen."

"Seems like a reasonable request."

"There are also some people I want to visit. People I haven't talked to in a while."

"Like Mrs. Briggs."

"Yes."

"Why?"

"That is the part I'd like to keep to myself."

"Gotcha. So we're off to Jake's then."

"Yep."

Kaylee turns the key in the ignition and shifts Candy into drive.

"Wait—one more thing," I say, pulling my camera out of my pocket.

"What?"

"We need a picture first," I say.

Kaylee leans in close, puts her arm around me. I breathe

her in, smell the chewing gum in her mouth, and imagine tasting it on her lips before shaking that thought off. I hold my arm out and take a self-portrait of us. Looking at the screen, I see Kaylee made a goofy face behind me and held bunny ears over my head. So immature, yet so cute.

"Let me see," she says, grabbing for the camera.

"No. Later," I tell her. She pouts but pulls away from the curb and heads to Jake's.

Jake Briggs lived north of Forty-Eighth Street on the west side of Pearl. Although his neighborhood is only a couple miles from our own, it's what I guess you would call the other side of the tracks—houses a little smaller, yards a little less manicured, kids a little tougher. White trash is what others call it, though I don't like the term myself.

Jake was the third of our trio. He and I had been friends since kindergarten, and he gladly accepted Kaylee when she started coming around. We had other friends, but the three of us were pretty much inseparable. I don't remember how Jake and I came together, really; we must have just clicked. We could just talk and laugh for hours at a time about nothing at all.

Everybody loved Jake. He was funny, smart; there wasn't anything *not* to like. Girls loved him; he was good-looking, had cool hair—as Kaylee would say, he was hot. Plus, he was good at everything: drama, music, soccer, but especially skateboarding. His skateboard was a part of him, like some freakish growth. Jake idolized Tony Hawk, spent much of his free time at the skate park, and had tons of awards proving his talent.

He had loads of practice time, being an only child to a single mom who worked more than she parented, out of necessity rather than choice. Sixteen years old, unmarried, she was abandoned by Jake's dad when she was pregnant. She had no choice but to get a job and depend on friends and family until Jake was old enough to unlock the front door himself. When he wasn't hanging out with Kaylee and me, he was out late riding that damn skateboard. Unfortunately, that thing he loved the most had a hand in his death.

One Friday night, about two years ago, Kaylee and I had gone to Jake's to watch a movie, more than likely *Superbad*. What can I say? We're freaks. I remember the movie ended pretty late. When we left, Jake followed us out with his skateboard.

"What are you doing?" I asked.

"I'm just going to go out for a bit until my mom gets home."

"Jake, that's crazy," Kaylee said. "It's dark."

"I do it all the time, Kaylee. Look, I've even got reflectors on my coat *and* my board. I'm not stupid, you know."

"Just be careful," she said.

He just laughed and rode off down the street.

"I'm serious!" she called after him. He waved over his shoulder and flipped us off.

Ten minutes later he was hit by a car that never slowed down and never turned back.

We pull up to the curb outside of Jake's house. Kaylee begins to open her door. I touch her shoulder gently. "Um, Kaylee," I say.

"Yeah?"

"This is something I'd like to do alone. Do you mind waiting in the car?"

"Oh, no, sure, go ahead," she answers, though she sounds pissed.

"I'm not sure how long I'll be."

"Whatever." She puts her ear buds in place and turns on her iPod. She sticks her tongue out at me when I go to close the car door.

I knock on the door of the little rundown blue house at the end of a dead-end street. Too early for visiting most people, but because of Susan Briggs's work schedule, this is the best time to catch her home.

When Mrs. Briggs answers the door, she looks down to

the ground and says, "Austin. What are you doing here?" I don't mind. I understand why she can't look at me.

"Can I come in?" I ask.

"Sure, for a bit. I have to get ready for work soon," she answers, gesturing me forward.

The stench of stale cigarettes almost makes me gag. The shades are drawn, darkness cast across everything like a ghostly shadow. I scan the living room, barely recognizing the place that used to be my second home. Once a small, clean sanctuary, now it is strewn with overflowing ashtrays, and dishes cover the counters and fill the sink. Pizza and takeout boxes litter the floor. No, it's not the place I remember.

"How have you been?" I trace my fingers along a picture of Jake and his mom, leaving a trail on the dust-caked frame.

She scans the room herself, an implication that the state of things should answer my question. She answers out loud anyway. "Oh, about the same. You know, hanging in there. Do you want something to drink? Coffee? Water? That's pretty much all I've got around here."

"No, thanks, I'm good . . . So, how's work going?" I ask, stalling, still unsure what I'm going to say. She doesn't buy it.

"What do you want, Austin?" she asks in a tired voice.

I don't want to answer her question, not yet. If I do, she'll tell me to leave, to mind my own business, and that's something I don't want to do. I want to talk to her, to make her understand, and I don't want to fail.

"Can I see Jake's room?"

"Jake's room?"

"Yes, can I?"

Mrs. Briggs exhales and then gestures for me to follow. She leads me down the short hallway to the room at the end. Hanging on the door is a sign that Jake made out of his first skateboard after it finally fell apart from years of abuse. The sign is hand-painted with skulls and crossbones, and reads BEWARE THE JAKE.

Mrs. Briggs places her hand on the knob and hesitates. Her pained expression makes me realize how difficult it must be for her to go in his room. I put a hand on her shoulder, and she twitches as if startled. Nodding, she turns the handle and opens the door, allowing me to enter Jake's room, while she remains in the doorway.

A forgotten shrine to a dead boy, the room is just how I remember. Music and girlie posters cover the walls; soccer and skateboarding trophies sit on the shelves. I walk in slowly, as not to disturb the dust and cobwebs. Jake's bed is unmade, as if he slept there the night before.

"May I?" I ask, motioning toward his CD collection. She again nods silently. I scan the discs, running my fingers across them as I read the names of Jake's favorite performers aloud:

the Beatles, AC/DC, the Smiths, Incubus, Kanye—an eclectic assortment, for sure. Rage Against the Machine. I pull that one from the shelf. "This was his favorite," I say, showing his mom.

"I hated it," she says. Tears well up in her eyes.

I put the CD back in its place and move over to his dresser, its mirror plastered with pictures—memories of every important event in Jake's short life, and some of the not-so-important ones as well.

"Did you take this?" I ask her, pointing to one of the pictures. She nods. "It was his first skateboarding competition, right?" Again, she just nods. "And here's our soccer team the year we went to state. And this one," I add, pointing to another. Mrs. Briggs finally enters the room to get a closer look. "This was the fifth grade talent show. Jake and I did that rap song. Do you remember?"

"How could I forget? I had to hear that stupid song every day for two months. You guys were awful, by the way." She laughs.

"Yeah, I know. The audience actually booed us off the stage, but we had a blast."

"How did that song go again?" she asks. She appears to be digging deep for the memory.

I think it over a moment. It had been a while. "Jake's part was first," I say, finally able to pull the memory from my own cranial depths. "My name is Jake / don't wear it out / girls and skateboarding's what I'm about. Then it was my turn. My name is Austin, and if you think / that I'm a loser, well then you stink." I laugh at how stupid it was.

"It's worse than I remember. Dreadful. Inane, really," Mrs. Briggs says as if reading my mind.

"Jake was such a good friend, so fun to be around, so cool. I miss him."

"I miss him too," she says. She examines the pictures as if seeing them for the first time. She inhales deeply, I'm not sure why. Maybe she's trying to draw in just a hint of anything Jake might have left behind.

"You know he'd want you to be happy, right?"

"Yes. I know."

"You should think about it." Mrs. Briggs is like a second mother to me, and I wouldn't want my own mother to give up on life the way she has.

She nods and begins to cry hard, which makes me think she hasn't done it in a while, but I know I'm probably wrong. Not really knowing what to do, I put my arms around her, not saying anything, just allowing her to let it out. I hold her until she calms, relaxes. She steps back, straightens out her shirt, stares at the tearstains she's left behind, and says, "Sorry, Austin."

"It's okay, Mrs. Briggs."

"I really need to finish getting ready for work now."

"Okay."

She looks at me thoughtfully, then grabs the picture of the talent show and the Rage Against the Machine CD. She hands them to me and says, "He would want you to have these."

I smile and say, "This means a lot to me." It must be hard for her, entering this room, disrupting it, giving part of it away.

She walks me to the door, shows me out. I thank her, and leave her to her life, hoping that she will indeed have one.

chapter five

"So, what did you do in there?" Kaylee asks as soon as I shut the car door.

"Just talked," I answer.

"Talked? About what?"

"It's personal," I say. She looks at me as if I've just punched her in the gut. I know I've hurt her feelings—we're best friends and tell each other everything—but I think if I talk about it I might break down. I held it together for Mrs. Briggs, but I don't think I could for another second. It's been two years, but it's still hard, especially now.

"Well, how did it go?" she asks.

"Good, I think." I slide the talent show picture inside Kaylee's car's sun visor.

"Oh my God, I remember that day," she says. "You guys were so horrible; I pretended I didn't know you. That was truly embarrassing." She turns the key in the ignition, sparking Candy back to life.

"Thanks a lot," I reply, slipping the CD into the player. I go straight to track number two, "Bulls on Parade," Jake's favorite.

Kaylee laughs when the music starts. "Oh my God!" she squeals. "I haven't heard this song in forever. I always hated it. It sounds so angry."

She's silent for a moment, listens intently to the rough, metallic chords as if hearing the song through new ears. She sighs and says, "I guess it's not that bad. Where next?"

"I want to see Juliana."

"What if Ben's there?"

"He's not. I checked. I'm not stupid."

"Are you sure about that?"

"That I'm not stupid? Yeah, I'm sure."

Kaylee stares at me and shakes her head in disbelief.

"Oh," I say. I feel like an idiot. "You mean am I sure Ben isn't there." She grins and nods. "Yeah, I told you, I checked. He's with Kyle today, doing some football player stuff. Whatever that is."

"Let's go then," she says as she pulls out of the dead-end street and heads east down Forty-Eighth.

Juliana is my ex-girlfriend. Yes, I've always loved Kaylee, but when the person you love doesn't love you back, you make do. I made do with Juliana. We dated most of our freshman year. She's the first girl I really made out with, copped a feel, even got naked once or twice, but that's as far as it went—no actual sex. She's a nice girl, pretty, nice body, but totally lacking in self-confidence, which was a big turnoff. It's part of the reason I broke up with her. She drove me nuts with the clinginess, constantly trying to please me, and apologizing for every little thing. It wasn't worth the headache. Her boyfriend now, Ben, is a total dick. He treats her like shit and hits her. I know because he brags about it in the locker room after PE. And we all just sit around and listen. We don't say anything or do anything, thinking it's none of our business. I'm going to try to do something now, to make it my business. She doesn't deserve to be treated that way.

I exit the car, turn back to Kaylee, and say, half joking, "Leave it running, just in case."

I shut the door and it muffles Kaylee's cry of "Not funny, Austin!"

I ring the bell and wait. A few moments later Juliana answers the door.

"Hi, Juliana," I say.

"Austin!" She grabs my sleeve and pulls me into the living room. "What the hell are you doing here? Ben finds you here, he'll kill us both."

I shrug my sleeve from her grasp and say more harshly than I intend, "I just want to talk to you."

She looks out the front window, up and down the street, as if searching for some invisible eye, some Big Brother. "Does Kaylee have to sit out front? Can she go take a drive or something?" she asks.

"Ben's with Kyle, isn't he?"

"Well, yeah, but sometimes he's unpredictable. You know him."

"Fine." I pull out my cell, ring Kaylee, and tell her to take a few trips around the block, or maybe go to Starbucks. She lets out an exasperated sigh on the other end of the line but drives away anyway.

Juliana lets out a breath and her shoulders lower. She's relaxed, if only a little. "What do you want, Austin?" she asks. She keeps her back to me, her eyes on the street beyond the window.

I don't really know how to approach it. Can you just blurt out "I know your boyfriend beats you up"? I don't think so. I start out slow: "How've you been?"

"Good, I guess."

"Really?"

Now she turns toward me, eyes narrowed, brows furrowed, arms crossed over her chest. This won't be easy. She says, "Yes, Austin, really. Cut the shit. What's up?"

"I'm worried about you."

"Why?"

"Because of Ben. I know how he treats you, Juliana. What he does to you."

"Mind your own business, Austin."

"I care about you. He brags about it, you know. He's proud of the way, as he calls it, he keeps you in line."

"You lost your right to care when you broke up with me. What? You didn't want me, but you don't want anyone else to have me either?" She's getting angry, and her eyes well up with tears.

"It's not like that. You deserve better than to be treated the way Ben treats you."

"What? I don't deserve this?" She lifts her sleeve and shows a yellowing bruise right below her shoulder. "Or maybe you're referring to these." She lifts her shirt and turns her back, which is covered with more bruises, some old and yellowing like the one on her arm, some fresh and purple, as if from no longer than a couple hours ago.

"Jesus. Why do you let him do that to you?"

She doesn't have an answer. Stays silent.

"I'd like to help you," I tell her.

"I loved you, you know, Austin? You broke my heart."

"I never meant to hurt you."

"Well, you did. I never want to feel pain like that again. Ben loves me. He won't break my heart."

"But he might break your arm, or your nose. You don't need the kind of love he's offering. It's no good. It's dangerous. He could really hurt you, Juliana."

"I've heard enough. Get out."

"Come on. Let me help."

"Help? What can you possibly do?"

I haven't thought it through. I have no idea what to do. I hesitate a little too long.

"That's what I thought. I don't need your empty promises. He'd kill you anyway," she says. "And then he'd kill me. He already hates you because you're my ex. I don't need your help."

"You need to break up with him."

"Yeah, then what? Go into the Witness Protection Program?"

"You tell your parents, the school counselor."

"Fuck off, Austin."

"Fine. I'll go, but my offer still stands. If you need anything call."

"Buh-bye," she says as sarcastically as she can through the crying, the anger, the hurt. I leave, walk down to the corner, just in case, and call for Kaylee to pick me up.

chapter six

"What happened in there?" Kaylee asks, handing me a decaf white mocha. Her voice sounds weird. I can't place the tone. She sounds kind of mad, or—wait, could it be jealousy? She never did seem to like Juliana all that much.

"I just tried to talk some sense into her, tried to help."

"And did you? Help, I mean?"

"I don't know. I don't think so."

"I hope you didn't make things worse," Kaylee says.

"How would I have made it worse? Shit, Kaylee! Ben won't even know I was there. What's wrong with people? They just don't get it."

"Get what?"

I feel bad that I've raised my voice, but I struggle, every day. I struggle with the whys in life. Why her? Why him? Why me? And I know for some there's no good answer. I get frustrated with the things that are out of my control and I wonder why people don't deal with the things they can control. I take a breath, calm down. "Nothing, never mind," I say.

After a moment of silence, Kaylee asks, quietly, almost in a whisper, "Where to now?"

"Peggy's."

Kaylee turns to face me, one eyebrow raised, and asks, "Why?"

"Because I visit her every Saturday. I just want to pop by for a few."

"Really? That's so sweet. How did I never know this about you?"

"I'm a man of mystery. What can I say?"

"Whatever," she says.

I chuckle. "Just drive, Kaylee."

"Your wish is my command." She rolls her eyes at me. She's so cute when she rolls her eyes. Again, I want to kiss her, but I'm scared, such a chickenshit. She puts the car in drive and we head across town.

Peggy's house is one degree less than a mansion, its presence felt on either side by much smaller homes. This is as close to an estate as you will get in the city of Tacoma. Peggy's grandfather, the lumber king, built it with his own hands—oh, and the hands of fifty employees.

"Should I stay out in the car again?" Kaylee asks.

"Do you mind? I'll only be a minute."

"Nope, I don't mind," Kaylee says as I once again step from the car.

I take the front steps slowly, counting each one as I cross. I always wondered but never counted how many steps led to that deep red front door. What seemed like a million when I was younger now seems to be only maybe, I don't know, five hundred thousand.

Three sets . . . six, seven . . . next set, fourteen, fifteen . . . last set, thirty-five, thirty-six. When I reach the top, my lungs feel as though they'll burst. I can't imagine Peggy being able to walk these steps much longer. She doesn't take very good care of herself; she eats like crap, sits on her ass all day, and drinks way too much. But what does she care? She's got money. It bugs me when people don't take care of their bodies, because sometimes your body doesn't take care of you.

I bend over, hands on my knees, to catch my breath. Kaylee leans over in her car, peers out the passenger window, checks on me, making sure I don't collapse. I try to smile between gasps, reassure her. She doesn't buy it. She darts out of the car and sprints up the stairs, taking them two at a time, and is by my side within seconds. Showoff. She rubs my back. "Are you okay?"

"Yeah, I'm fine," I say. I straighten up, take a breath.

She puts an arm around me. "I'm coming in," she says. There was no point in arguing. I would only lose.

A few more steps up the massive porch and we're in front of

the giant red door I've stood in front of so many times before. Big red doors seem a bit ostentatious to me, but it suits Peggy's big, boisterous personality. I ring the bell; it chimes Beethoven's *Für Elise*. I only know this because Peggy told me. I can't stand classical music. I tell Kaylee, "If I had a musical doorbell, it would play 'New Slang' by the Shins. That'd be cool."

"Mine would play 'Lollipop.'"

"What's that? Never heard of it."

"Lil Wayne? 'Lollipop'?"

"Nope."

"You don't listen to the radio much, do you?"

"Not really."

Helen, Peggy's housecleaner, answers the door. She's actually more like a companion than a housecleaner, and not in a gay way, just in a friendship way, a best friend way. She's been around for as long as I can remember.

"Good morning, Austin." She greets me with a peck on the cheek. "Come in." I'm no farther than the entryway when Peggy blasts in like a tornado through a mobile home.

"Austin!" Peggy greets me with a bear hug. She's crushing me, and it hurts, but it also feels good to be hugged like that. I remember being afraid of her when I was younger. She's huge, the size of a car, or so it seemed when I was little. She's not a very pretty woman, her face always overly painted with makeup. And she's loud, so loud. I grew out of my fear, grew to love her. Of course, she bribed me with cookies, and I think children will do anything for cookies.

"Nice to see you," she says upon releasing me. "Ah, you've brought Kaylee with you."

"Hi," Kaylee says. Peggy ushers us out of the open foyer, through the fancy-schmancy living room and the pretentiously decorated dining room, and straight to the chrome kitchen. She's very proud of her décor, can talk for hours about it, and has on occasion. She's put me to sleep a few times over it.

Peggy automatically grabs a plate, places four cookies on it, and pours two glasses of milk, just as she does every time I visit. Kaylee and I sit down at the counter.

"So, Austin, how are you doing?" she asks. She places her elbows on the counter and leans in as if I'm the most interesting person on the face of the earth.

"Some days are good. Some aren't. Today is okay. How about you?"

"Some days are good. Some aren't. Today is better now that you're here," she says. "I'm getting old, you know. Gravity and pain are taking me over."

"You're not that old. You can't be a day over forty," I tease, knowing full well that she's at least sixty-five.

"Oh, Austin, you little charmer, you. You sure know how

to make an old lady feel young again. You look good," she says as she eyes me up and down. "Doesn't he look good?" she asks Helen, who has just trailed us into the kitchen.

"Oh, yeah, real good," Helen says, though she barely looks at me. I can tell she's lying.

"Such a handsome young man," Peggy compliments.

"Thanks," I say. I feel my face redden, even though I know that's just something old ladies say.

"Tell me what's going on with you. What are you two up to today?"

"I have some things I need to take care of these next couple of days. Kaylee's agreed to drive me around."

Peggy nods and wears an expression that I've been witness to too much lately. Profound sadness. I've seen it at home, in the hallways at school, when I hang out with friends. I can't get used to it. And sometimes? It just plain pisses me off.

Kaylee and I eat the cookies while Peggy tells stories of her latest vacation to Rome. There's never a quiet moment when Peggy's around, which is fine with me. I love listening to her talk, hearing her stories about old times and distant places. My weekly visits with her are a nice distraction.

When the cookies are gone and the story ends, I say, "We have a lot to do. We really gotta go."

She walks us to the door, and while she gives me another crushing hug, I say, "Will you do me a favor?"

She backs off, yet still clings to my shoulders. "Well, of course. Anything for you."

"Will you call your daughter?"

"I don't know about that, Austin," she answers.

"I need you to. Please?"

She stares at me a minute, then says, "Yes, of course."

"Thanks, Peggy. See you soon?"

"Of course you will." She looks in my eyes and adds, "And would it kill you to call me Grandma?"

I smirk. "No, of course not. Goodbye, Grandma," I say. It's kind of funny, yet I find myself feeling sentimental, close to tears.

She releases me from her grasp, smiles, and says, "I love you, Austin."

I return the smile. "I love you too, Grandma." She watches us out the door, off the porch, down the steps, all the way into Kaylee's car. She waves as we drive away.

"You okay? You look kind of soft and mushy," Kaylee asks.

I laugh away any sentiment I felt. "Shut up and drive."

"I'm kind of driving aimlessly at the moment. Where to now?"

"The fair."

"The fair? We're going to the fair?"

"Yeah, just for a little while. I have a couple of things I want to do there."

"Do I get to get out of the car again?" she asks.

"Of course."

"Well, I wouldn't want to presume," she says in a snobby voice.

"Kaylee, I need you there. I'm going to need some moral support."

"Moral support, huh? Okay, I'm in," she says. She turns left and heads to the freeway.

The Puyallup Fair comes just once a year a couple weeks after school starts. It's one of the most attended events in all of Pierce County, Washington. Rides, food, rodeo, exhibits, and concerts—you could spend an entire week there. However, I have only one reason for going to the fair this year: to face my fears.

chapter seven

There we stand, looking toward the sky, up to the grand tower above us. "You sure you want to do this?" Kaylee asks.

"Uh, yeah. I think. I mean, yes, definitely," I say, looking up at the most frightening thing at the Puyallup Fair, the Extreme Scream, the ultimate experience in speed and height, the latter of which I'm terrified.

The line is long, as always. This ride alone costs ten bucks, a small price to pay to face your greatest fear, get past it, move forward. Twenty stories high, thrusting at three Gs on the way up, negative one on the way down, this ride has haunted me for years. Friends have stood in this very line every year, teasing me, begging me to ride with them. Me, I'm always too scared to join them. Not this year, not anymore.

Kaylee grabs my shaking hand and lays her head on my arm in comfort. My heart races, from both the anticipation of the ride and Kaylee's warmth beside me. She smells like cherry, not the real fruit cherry smell, but that processed cherry scent you find in shampoo, and lip balm, and Life Savers. I'd like to kiss her lips right now and see if they taste like cherry too, but I'm so nervous already, the thought makes me want to throw up.

The line moves so slowly, as if mocking me, trying to get me to give up, to leave. Not gonna happen. I watch as the riders before me shoot up into the air, hair flying, screaming, and know I'll be screaming like a girl when it's my turn.

We finally get to the front of the line. I set my camera to video and ask a woman who reminds me of my mother if she'll film our ride. She agrees. Kaylee and I remove our shoes and put them in the cubbyholes, find two empty seats next to each other, and strap ourselves in. Kaylee grabs my hand again, assuring me that I won't die, right here, on the Extreme Scream. The ride attendants come by and check everyone's harnesses, belts, and buckles to make sure they're secure. Like that's going to help if my seat flies up and off the tracks, shoots into the air, out over the ride, and then plummets down onto the pavement beneath, killing me instantly. I try to push that thought from my mind.

The countdown begins . . . ten, nine, eight . . . Kaylee lets go of my hand and grabs on to her harness. I give her my best "What the hell?" look and she giggles. Seven, six, five . . . I'm now aware of the need to hold on for dear life, so I too grab my harness with a death grip . . . four, three, two . . . I close my eyes, breathe in, breathe out, breathe in. One . . . we shoot up the tower at what feels like the speed of light. I feel helpless, dangling, with no control of my limbs. Just as I thought, I scream like a little girl, flailing, and praying to God I don't piss my pants. The ride stops as suddenly as it started, at the top of the tower. I open my eyes, take in the view of the fairgrounds below me, trying desperately not to freak out. When we plunge back down, my stomach drops to my knees and my mouth goes dry. Up and down again, up and down, slowing with each phase, until the ride finally ends and we are safely back on the earth. I'm finally able to let out my breath. I want to lie face-down and hug the ground, thank it for being so solid, and still.

When my feet hit the earth, my knees buckle and I nearly collapse. Kaylee and one of the attendants grab me and hold me up.

"You okay, man?" the attendant asks. He looks just like a fair attendant should, big, bald, missing some teeth, a cliché tattoo on his gigantic bicep—MOM in a red heart. I'm sure if he were to bend over, we'd get a view of his butt crack as well. He reeks of cigarettes and whiskey, disconcerting for someone who has just put his life in this man's hands. The stench makes me nauseous. I run to a nearby garbage can and puke, a horrible waste of cookies.

Kaylee looks at me and can't help but laugh at my expense. I wipe my mouth and laugh with her.

"Is it everything you thought it would be?" she asks.

"And more," I answer.

I grab my camera from the woman and we walk around for a bit, check out the exhibits and the animals to let my stomach settle. When I'm ready I say, "Let's get lunch."

"Lunch?" She chuckles. "You sure? Are you ready?"

"Yeah, I'm starved; I just lost my breakfast and cookies all in one shot." She laughs again. I love making her laugh. Her dimples show, her cheeks turn red. Just a second of her laughter can get me through my darkest day. We head toward the food vendors.

"What will it be?" Kaylee asks. "Earthquake Burger? Krusty Pup? Or do you want to go straight to dessert with an elephant ear, deep-fried Twinkie, or a scone? Name your grease-ridden-fatty-heart-attack-waiting-to-happen food of choice."

"I want that," I say, pointing to the Barbecue Pete's booth.

"Sounds good to me. I loves me some barbecue," she says.

We head over to the booth, built to resemble an Old West saloon. Kaylee orders some chicken and corn on the cob. She steps aside to let me order.

"I'd like some buffalo chicken wings, that chipotle

coleslaw, an order of fries . . . oh, and the largest Coke you've got."

"Are you crazy?" Kaylee says laughing. "You hate hot!"

"I want to see how much I can take. I want to feel the burn. You only live once, you know." Kaylee looks at me with sad eyes. We grab our food and head to an open table.

She digs right in to her chicken, but I hesitate, a bit apprehensive about the heat I'm getting ready to stick in my mouth. Do I want to begin with the hottest item on my plate, which I imagine is the buffalo chicken, or should I start with the coleslaw and ease my way into the hot? The Coke and fries are strictly for balance.

"What are you waiting for? Let the pain begin," she says, corn kernels flying out of her mouth.

"I think I'll start with the chicken," I say.

"Your funeral," she says. She looks into my face; I smile, instantly easing her discomfort. She smiles back sweetly.

"Here, you have to film it." I hold out the Cyber-shot to her. She wipes her hands, then aims the camera.

I pick up a piece of the chicken, study it carefully, take a lick of the sauce with the very tip of my tongue, grimace, and put it back down on my plate. "This is not going to be easy," I joke.

"You wuss. Just do it." She giggles as she says it.

"Okay. Here it goes." I pick the chicken back up and

quickly tear off a piece of the well-soaked, saucy meat. I chew quickly, the heat radiating quickly from my tongue to the sides and top of my mouth to the back of my throat. My face heats up and I could swear my eyeballs are sweating. I swallow, fanning my hand in front of my mouth until I get ahold of my Coke. I take a huge swig.

"You should see your face, Austin. It's classic," Kaylee says.

"Holy shit, that was hot!" I yell, earning disapproving looks from all the parents within earshot.

I take a few deep breaths, and after my mouth cools down a bit, I reach for my fork and dig in to the coleslaw.

"Are you crazy?" Kaylee asks. "You're still going to try that even after the chicken?"

"I'm on a mission—what can I say?" I look at the fork briefly, inhale deeply, and shove it into my mouth. I chew, once again as quickly as possible. I couldn't have been more wrong. The slaw is about four times hotter than the chicken. Heat travels from my head down through my internal organs and out to my limbs. Surely flames will shoot out my fingers and toes at any second. My lips as well as the inside of my mouth are in a painful blaze. I wouldn't be surprised if the whites of my eyes glowed red. I down the rest of my soda and push the hot items toward Kaylee.

"They're all yours," I say as I pull the fries toward me and shove one in my mouth.

Kaylee, a bottomless pit, has already eaten her chicken and corn, yet eats my wings and slaw without incident. She then helps me with my fries, licks her lips, and lets out a big burp.

"Nice rip," I compliment.

"Thanks."

"A couple more rides, then we head out?" I ask.

"Sure."

There are only two I want to go on, the first being the roller coaster. When you go to the fair, it's blasphemous not to hit the roller coaster at least once. It's my favorite ride. I love the way the wind hits your face, and the anxiousness you feel as you climb the hills, the way your stomach plummets into your bowels on the way down. It makes you feel young, alive, free. It's easy to lose yourself, to forget, on the roller coaster.

My other choice is the haunted house. I don't scare easily, but I know Kaylee does. It's not the visuals that make a haunted house. True, it's scary when things jump out at you, but not half as scary without the sound effects—the moaning, the screaming, the creaking. That's the difference between scary and terrifying.

We climb into our car and pull the lock down. It jerks to life, heads down the track, and through the double doors.

It's dark, so dark we can't even see each other. An ugly mummified face shoots out at us. I feel Kaylee's body twitch as she screams. I can't help but laugh.

"Austin!" she screams, and slugs me in the arm.

Face after hideous, chilling, menacing face comes at us, and Kaylee's body shudders and jolts with each one. I put my arm around her and pull her in. She lays her head down on my shoulder and takes my other hand in hers on my lap. I feel my body start to react to her; my heart feels as though it will tear through my chest. I turn toward her; she's so close, I can hear her breathe. I kiss the top of her head. She shifts beside me. Through the green, blue, and black lights, I see her turn her face up toward mine. I bend in for that kiss I've waited so long for. Just as our lips are about to join, our car bursts through the doors at the end of the ride, an ambush of bright sun blinding us.

We quickly jump back from and stare at each other for a moment. Then Kaylee bursts out laughing. I follow suit, though I'm really dying inside. Being so close to that kiss . . . it's heartbreaking. I guess sometimes people will do things in the dark that maybe they won't in the light.

We continue, though it's hard for me to concentrate, but it's Kaylee's turn to pick rides. She likes the spinning ones, so after enjoying (or not) rides such as the Matterhorn, the

Zipper, the Enterprise, and the Octopus, I'm done. I have to put my foot down at the Ferris wheel.

"You ready to go?" I ask. I've had enough "fun" at the fair.

"If you are." We head out of the fairgrounds and back to Candy, who is patiently waiting in the straw-covered parking lot to take us to our next stop.

chapter eight

"Next destination?" Kaylee asks.

"Allie."

"Jesus, Austin."

"Kaylee, can you please just try to understand?"

She stares into my eyes with . . . I don't know what: maybe sympathy, maybe insight. She's so beautiful. I think again about our almost-kiss, what I wouldn't give to do it all over. If I had only put my arm around her earlier. Sometimes my stupidity amazes even me. I'd try again, but when she laughed, it was as if it were all some terrible joke. Maybe I misread her, though. Maybe I'll try again later. *Yes, later,* I promise myself. She puts the key in the ignition, lets out a large sigh, and starts the car.

She doesn't speak all the way to Allie's house; I wonder what she's thinking. She probably thinks I'm nuts to try to do all of this in a day, or the weekend, however long it takes. Deep down I know she gets it. She gets my need to fix things that have broken along the way, to mend fences. Maybe if we all just tried to put the pieces back together as soon as they fell out of place, the puzzles in our lives would feel more like an accomplishment than a chore.

Kaylee pulls up to the curb in front of Allie's house. I turn to get out of the car, but Kaylee stops me. "Are you sure about this one?" she asks.

"I'm sure."

"She's not the same, you know. She's not the Allie we used to know."

"Yes, she is. Deep down, I think she is. I want to try to bring *that* Allie out again."

"What if you can't, Austin? You can't help everyone."

"At least I'll know I tried."

"I sure hope you know what you're doing," she says.

"I don't. But I know what I'm trying to do. Is that good enough?"

"I don't know, Austin. Just go. Go about your business. I'll be sitting here in the car, alone, if you need me."

I exit the car, head up the walk to the front door, and ring the bell. Allie answers. She's definitely not the Allie I used to know. That Allie was cute, lively, fun, and a bit fat. This Allie is dark, depressed, gaunt, and thin. Too thin.

"Austin, dude, what are you doing here?" she says. She reeks of pot.

"I wanted to see you."

"See me? Why? I mean, no offense, but we haven't exactly been best buds for a while."

"That was your choice," I remind her.

"So it was." She nods. "Who's in the car?" She motions toward Candy.

"Kaylee."

"Are you guys like boyfriend-girlfriend now?"

"No, just friends."

She eyes Kaylee out in the car as if trying to see something more than I've told her. She always did have a keen intuition, a knack for reading people. She looks back to me, gives a knowing look, nods, and says, "Why is she waiting in the car?"

"Because I asked her to."

She looks at me suspiciously now. I think maybe she'll turn me away. Instead she says, "Come in.

"I'd offer you something to drink or eat, but the cupboards are pretty bare. Mom doesn't shop worth a shit anymore, and, well, you know my dad's never home. You want to sit?"

"Sure." I take a seat on the couch. She sits down next to me. I survey the room carefully. It looks the same—the country décor, the pig collection in the corner—but there's something different about it, something not quite right. The air. I don't mean oxygen; I mean atmosphere. It's suffocating, as if at any moment I'll be gasping for breath. I shake it off, get down to the reason I'm here.

"So, how've you been, Allie?"

She stares at me blankly, as if I've not said anything at all. An awkward silence hangs between us. She finally speaks. "You know how I've been, Austin. I've been shit." She reaches over to the side table and grabs a little plastic bag. She takes a pill from the bag and begins to scrape the outer coating off with her fingernail. "So, what's up, Austin? Why are you here? What's with the visit?"

I'm mesmerized by her actions. She wraps the scraped pill in a piece of paper and places it on the coffee table in front of us. Grabbing a lighter, she pounds it on the paper over and over. "Austin?"

I look up at her and she's staring at me. I momentarily forget the purpose of my visit. "A lot of people miss you, Allie."

"Miss me?" She carefully unfolds the paper, revealing the pill, which is now nothing but a fine powder. "I see everyone at school every day; they don't miss me. I walk through the halls by myself, eat lunch by myself, sit in class by myself." Allie places lines of the powder in front of her and proceeds to snort them through a straw. Her eyes water as she wipes residue from under her nose and licks her finger.

Not able to help myself any longer, I ask, "What is that?"

She looks up and simply says, "OC," then snorts another line.

"OC?" I ask, feeling stupid.

"OxyContin."

"Do you have a prescription for that?" The look she gives me answers my question.

She continues our conversation without a second thought. "Austin, if everyone misses me so much, why don't they come over and say so?" She pauses shortly, then says, "I'm a ghost, Austin, nothing more than a ghost."

"You haven't exactly made yourself approachable lately. Plus, that's not what I'm talking about. I mean, they miss the old Allie, that Allie you used to be, before, well, you know," I say.

She looks right through me. "That Allie doesn't exist anymore, Austin. That Allie is dead."

"She doesn't have to be," I say.

"Yes, she does. She belongs in a cold, dark place. This is where she lives now." She points to her head. "Up here, in an unmarked grave."

"Dig her back out," I say. She ignores me. More awkward silence, I'm struggling for the right words to make her see. "It could have happened to anyone," I blurt out.

"But it didn't happen to anyone, Austin. It happened to me."

"Do you want to talk about it?"

"No." She becomes visibly frustrated.

"Have you ever talked about it?"

"No." Now she gets angry.

"I think you should," I suggest.

Allie rises from the couch and yells, "No! No one wants to hear that story, Austin. What? Do you think this is some kind of fairy tale? This isn't a fairy tale. It's a nightmare. My nightmare. I think you should mind your own damn business! What the fuck?"

"I just want to help."

"You want to help? Give me a lobotomy so I don't remember. Put a gun to my head and pull the trigger. Please! I've wanted to a million times—I'm just too chicken to do it." She begins to cry as she collapses back onto the couch.

Her body trembles. She looks so fragile, so bony, like she could be easily broken. She cries, "It's just been so hard. My dad, he ignores me as if I don't even exist. When I try to talk to my mom, she shushes me and tells me I just need to get over it and on with my life. They don't even care! They see me as a disgrace, damaged goods, a stain on their picture-perfect family."

"I'm sure they don't," I try.

"Yes, they do!" she screams, eyes wild with turmoil, chest heaving with what must be painful gasps. She continues until her body tires, slows, comes to a stop.

"It was broad daylight," she begins her story. "Broad fucking daylight," she repeats. "I can't believe nobody saw, nobody heard anything. He snuck up behind me, scared the shit out of me. I'm sure I must have screamed, but now the memory's so fuzzy, I don't know if I'm remembering it right. I was walking down to the Circle K to buy some candy, like I did every Friday after school."

"I remember. You always had a major sweet tooth," I say.

She looks over at me as if she had forgotten that I was there. She continues. "Yeah, I loved it all, chocolate, gummies, caramel, Nerds, Starbursts, Skittles. I'd always come home with a huge bag, enough for the entire weekend. Enough to share with you guys." She looks at me with disgust, as if she's casting blame, though I know she holds the expression for the memory, not for me.

"He forced me into the bushes, where the old folks' community is now. I can't believe how fast that place went up." Her eyes drift for a moment as if lost in thought; then she comes back. "He pulled me in there and threw me down onto the fucking ground, right on top of the sticker bushes.

He put a hand over my mouth, the other held a knife to my throat. He said if I did what he wanted he wouldn't kill me. I just nodded like an idiot; I didn't even try to fight back. I was such a chicken."

"No, you weren't. You were scared," I say.

She glares at me, eyes still crazed. "Yes, I was. I should have fought him off or I should have died trying," she says, almost in a whisper.

"I stumbled home. There was so much blood. It got on my shoes. I loved those goddamn shoes; they were ruined."

"I'm so sorry, Allie."

"I tried to get back to normal after that, remember? Tried to hang, tried to forget. You tried to help, and Kaylee, I know. Don't think I didn't notice. But it was too much. Sometimes I wish he would have just killed me." Tears again fall. "And that's not all," she goes on. Although this is exactly what I have come here for, I'm not sure I want to hear any more, not sure I can take it. But I have to. I have her talking about it, something she's never done. I have to see it through.

"That fucker got me pregnant."

"Jesus, Allie, I didn't know," I say, shocked by this new information, heart now aching for my once good friend.

"No one knew that part. My world came crashing down. My dad continued to ignore it, ignore me. He couldn't even look at me. Still can't. My mom took me to get rid of what she called 'the abomination.' The old Allie died that day, on the sticker bushes, right along with her virginity and her self-respect. Sex is an act of love? What a fucking joke. Painful and ugly, that's what it is. And don't even show me a piece of candy—I'll ram it down your fucking throat. I don't touch it anymore, haven't eaten a piece since."

"It looks like you don't eat much of anything. Do you?"

"Sometimes. I usually get rid of it though."

"Get rid of it?" I ask, immediately regretting my ignorance.

"Yeah, get rid of it. Stick my finger down my throat, puke it up," she replies.

"Why?"

"Because it feels good. It feels good to force it out, like I'm ridding myself of everything, everything bad, everything toxic that's ever touched me, been inside me. I was so stupid, such a fat cow. I just had to have that damn candy. If it weren't for that candy, none of this would have happened."

"It might have," I say. "Another day, another place, another girl. It wasn't about you or your candy habit. It was about some psycho fuck that gets off on hurting people. You should get help. You're slowly killing yourself, you know."

"I don't care. No one cares. Anyway, like I said, I'm already dead."

"I care, Allie. That's why I'm here. And you shouldn't choose death. It'll come for you soon enough."

Allie turns her eyes toward mine, glossed over from drugs and tears. "I don't know how to live anymore, Austin, how to be normal, how to deal. I only know how to get numb, how to purge. I don't even remember that fat girl that used to be me, and you're talking about getting her back? I wouldn't even know where to start."

"Forgiveness," I tell her.

"Forgive who? That fucking rapist in the bushes who took everything from me?"

"No. You start by forgiving yourself."

"Myself?"

"Yes, you can't blame yourself for what's happened to you. It's not your fault."

"Why does it feel like it is?"

"I don't know, maybe because the people around you made you feel that way by not hearing you, or seeing you, so it's been building up inside, eating away at you. You try to rid yourself of it through eating disorders and addictions. I want Allie back. My Allie. Fun, cool, totally hilarious Allie. I think she's still in there, dying to get out. You need to talk to someone—a counselor, your doctor, me, anyone you think can help."

"What if I just want to die?"

"Then I will be sad and disappointed that you cheated yourself out of your chance at existence. Not all of us have that opportunity, you know, to choose life."

She sits, nodding at nothing in particular, then says, "Why do you care so much? I mean, no one else seems to."

I have to think for a minute. It's hard to put into words what's been driving me this weekend. I wasn't sure I even understood it. Then I say, "Because I'm looking at the world through new eyes, that's why. And I don't like everything I'm seeing. I guess I'm also a little jealous."

She looks at me. "Jealous?" she says.

"Yes. You have a chance to live and breathe. Take it. You never know when that life, that breath, is going to be snatched away." We sit in silence for a moment, and then I stand to leave. "I've got to go now, Allie. Are you okay?"

She looks up at me, nods again. "Yeah, I'm okay. Thanks for coming by. I appreciate it. Tell Kaylee I said hey."

"Sure," I say. I try to read her face, to see if maybe I had gotten through to her. It's hard to tell. I leave. She doesn't get up, doesn't walk me to the door, just sits, nodding, thinking. I did what I came to do, did my best. It's all I can do.

I get into the car and tell Kaylee to drive. Once we're down the street, I cry. Maybe it was too much, seeing Allie, hearing her story, being a witness to her loneliness, her sadness. For the first time that day, I feel truly overwhelmed.

chapter nine

"How could someone do that to her?" I cry. "To Allie? He ruined her, Kaylee. He fucking ruined her. I don't know if she'll ever be the same."

Kaylee pulls over, stops the car. "Austin, we should go home."

I ignore her. "How can you do that to another human being? People like that selfish fuck, they don't understand. They don't see how valuable a person's life is! He treated her like a *thing*, Kaylee. Something to be used and just thrown away like a fast food wrapper."

"Austin, I really think I should take you home."

"No!" My tears are still flowing. My mind is beginning to disagree with my mouth. I think maybe she's right. Maybe it's too much. I wonder if I'm really making any kind of difference at all. I throw my head back onto the headrest, shut my eyes, breathe deep. Reevaluate. Kaylee stays quiet. I decide. "No," I repeat.

She unbuckles, slides over, wraps her arms around me. I lay my head on her chest. Her hair tickles my head and face. I listen to her heartbeat, listen to her breathe. God I love her! But I know I'll never have her, and it kills me. She holds me closer still. I don't want the moment to end, but I know it has to. I still have much to do.

I let the tears dry, then sit up, calm down. "Thanks." I gaze into those beautiful blue eyes. Eyes so bright, they're almost blinding, like looking directly into the sun.

"That's what friends are for," she says. Her choice of words makes me sad, but the label fits, friendship being all we've ever had.

"So, what do you want to do?" she asks once I'm calm.

"I want to keep going," I say.

"Are you absolutely sure? That seemed kind of rough," she says.

"It was worth it. I'm sure."

"Okay, so, where are we going?"

"Seattle," I answer.

"Sweet," she says, then hesitates. "There will be some fun involved, right? It won't be more fear and tears, will it?"

"All fun," I answer.

"Great!"

"With maybe just a little fear," I add.

She drops an eyebrow. "Well, then let the fear and fun begin," she says while turning the key, reigniting Candy, who in turn sparks and sputters and then calms to a dull roar.

Kaylee flips on the radio for the first time that day. She pushes buttons until she finds a song she likes. She sings. It's a song about a girl named Shawty slapping her own ass. "What *is* this?" I ask.

"You've never heard this song?"

I look at her and shake my head. "Never heard it before. That's not real music anyway," I say as I begin to push the buttons on her stereo.

"Hey! My car, my music," she says.

I keep pushing buttons. "Kaylee, seriously, let me find an actual song with music and lyrics and meaning. Why do I care if Shawty's slapping her ass or whatever? You'll thank me later. Trust me." I flip until I hear a song I know. It's just starting, which is good, because it's one of my favorites. "Now, this is music," I say.

It's one of my favorite bands. The singer sings of love and death, and I hum along and smile. I turn to look at Kaylee, to ask her what she thinks. She's facing forward, ramrod straight, watching the freeway ahead, tears streaming down her face. "Turn it off," she says.

"But, Kaylee—"

"I said turn it off! Shit, Austin!" I comply without another word, and we sit in silence the rest the way to Seattle.

She parks the car and I reach into my wallet to pay for the spot. She gets out, puts the money in the proper slot, comes back to the car, and leans in. "Sorry," she says.

I get out myself, come around to her side, hug her, and say, "It's okay."

"That song was just so sad. It makes me think," she says.

"It's not sad. It's about two people being together for eternity. What's sad about that?"

She brushes away another tear forming in the corner of her eyes, rubs her nose, and says, "Nothing, I guess."

"Exactly. So are you ready to have some fun?"

"It's about time. What are we doing first?"

"EMP," I answer.

"Very cool. I've never been."

"Me either," I say.

The building looks like something out of a sci-fi movie: blue tile, purple and silver metallic squares reflecting the sun's blaring glare. We stop to take a self-portrait outside before entering.

It's the Experience Music Project, a museum dedicated to popular music, honoring the Seattle-bred musician Jimi

Hendrix and built by the cofounder of Microsoft Paul Allen. Standing in the center of the museum, we gaze up at the thirty-five-foot cyclone gracing the center of the room: *Roots and Branches,* a sculpture created out of a variety of musical instruments, including six hundred guitars.

We grab a couple of audio guides, which are really just glorified iPods. They explain the exhibits we'll be checking out.

We journey down the Northwest Passage, a hallway honoring all musicians that have come from the area and then head to the Guitar Gallery, an exhibit on the history of the guitar.

Next, we head upstairs to On Stage. Brought into a darkened fake concert stage, we get to pick our own instrument. Kaylee chooses the drums; I take the guitar and mike. You don't need any talent whatsoever—the instruments play themselves and you're only lip-synching to your song of choice, ours being "Wild Thing." They film the entire act, burn it to DVD, and photograph you for a concert poster. I buy both, for twenty-five bucks, a small price to pay to feel like a rock star for three minutes.

With so much to see and not much time, we go directly back downstairs to the Sky Church. If you ever want to be completely absorbed in music, the Sky Church is the place to be. It is a musical religious experience. Before us, a forty-by-seventy-foot video screen displays visions that seem channeled directly from some psychedelic dream. As the music flows from all different angles, it surrounds us, and we feel like we're swimming—no, being baptized—in music. We let it wash over us.

A video of Jimi singing "Little Wing" comes on, and I grab Kaylee's hand, spin her around, and pull her in to slow dance with me. I can tell she's embarrassed at first. Giggling, she tries to pull away. I bring her in closer, and she relents, resting her head on my chest. I realize we've never danced before and more than likely never will again. I want to stay there for hours, pressed in to her like that, smelling her hair, feeling her warmth on my chest, but we have other things to do. I reluctantly pull away. She looks up and smiles, and we move on.

Now done with our tour through the museum, we exit and collapse on a bench outside.

"Ready to head back?" Kaylee asks, looking incredibly tired, which is exactly how I'm feeling.

"Not yet." I look up toward that monument in the sky, the one that defines Seattle and its skyline.

Kaylee follows my gaze and smiles. "I've never been up there. You ever been up there?" she asks.

"Nope, never."

"Then what are we waiting for?" I shrug my shoulders and rise, and we walk toward the Space Needle.

Kaylee gets in line outside for the elevator ride. Secretly, I've already made reservations, so we have to check in at the front desk, which is good, because since it's a Saturday, the line is huge and I'm not sure how long I could have stood there, my legs weak, pain radiating from my feet to my back.

"I want to go ask a question inside. Come on," I say.

We get inside and I tell Kaylee to look around the gift shop while I check in. I don't want to ruin the surprise. Luckily, since she's never been here, she doesn't know the procedure. The elevator we'll be taking is for people with reservations for the restaurant. I motion her back over and we wait for the indoor elevator.

"Why are we taking this elevator?" she asks.

"Because it's here," I answer, hoping she doesn't question any more, which, thank God, she doesn't.

It takes what seems forever for the elevator to arrive. I hand my reservation card to the attendant and we load into the elevator with our fellow riders. I get the camera ready to take pictures of the journey upward. My stomach tangles in knots as we rise higher and higher into the sky. Kaylee grabs the camera and turns it on me, recording my terror. If this, along with the Extreme Scream, doesn't completely cure my fear of heights, nothing will.

The elevator stops just below the observation deck. The doors open and I grab Kaylee's hand and try to pull her out and into the SkyCity Restaurant. She yanks her hand away and says, "No, Austin, no way. It's too expensive."

"Kaylee, come on. We already have reservations. Haven't you always wanted to eat here? I know I have. Please?"

"Fine, but I'm paying for my own dinner."

"No, you're not."

"It's too much, Austin," she repeats as if I hadn't heard her the first time.

"Where else am I going to spend it?"

She looks up at me. I thought I would see those eyes full of understanding, kindness—pity, even. Instead, she glares at me, and I crack up, which I'm sure isn't the reaction she's looking for.

"I'm glad you think this is funny," she says, still giving me an icy glare.

"I don't, really, but you're so cute when you're mad," I slip.

She whips her head around, gives me a flirty smile, and overdramatically bats her lashes. "You think I'm cute?"

I turn it around with a joke: "Only when you're mad. Otherwise, you're hideous. I mean, come on, have you looked in a mirror lately? Stringy hair, practically skeletal, totally ugly." We both laugh. "Can we eat now? I'm starved. I mean, I haven't exactly had a square meal today," I say.

"Oh, that's right, the entire contents of your stomach aside from a few french fries was left in a Puyallup Fair trash can. You must be hungry. Okay, fine, we'll eat," she says, and we head toward the maitre d'. Seated by the window, we're able to enjoy the view to the fullest.

"Do you know what you want?" I ask.

Kaylee looks at the menu. "Christ, it's all so expensive!" she says. She immediately blushes when she realizes how loudly she's spoken. Several of our fellow patrons glance at us, frown, and whisper. I force myself not to crack up. Kaylee puts her menu down. "Order for me. I feel guilty enough eating here. I don't want to feel bad about ordering one of these fifty-dollar dinners."

The waiter arrives for our order. "We'll start with the prosciutto-wrapped Beecher's Flagship cheese and the Sky-City greens. The lady will have the oven-roasted Jidori chicken, and I'll have the petite Kobe top sirloin."

"Very good, sir. Anything to drink?"

I look over to Kaylee. She says, "Let's live it up. How about a Shirley Temple?"

"Two Shirley Temples, please." I hand the menus to the waiter and he leaves us.

"Have I told you you're crazy yet today?" Kaylee asks.

"At least twice." The waiter comes with our drinks, and as we're enjoying them I say, "Let's talk."

"About what?" Kaylee asks.

"Memories."

"Memories? Like what?"

"The day we met. Do you remember?"

"Yeah. I was on the swings and those two idiot boys tried to push me off."

I remember distinctly. Third grade. Even back then I knew there was something special about her. She stood out from everyone, like she glowed or something. I had been leaning against the cool metal of the swing set, just staring at her. Until those two assholes came by.

"And I came to your rescue," I say.

"I didn't need you to come to my rescue." Kaylee laughs. "You were showing off. Trying to be all macho."

"They left you alone, didn't they?"

"You were about a foot taller than they were. I can't say I blame them."

"True. And I was mean."

"Never to me," she says, making me blush, though I'm not sure why.

While talking and waiting for our food, we check out the view of Seattle and beyond. The building spins so slowly, it's barely noticeable. Thank God for a clear day. We can see two bodies of water from our window, Elliott Bay and Lake Washington, the latter being the second-largest natural lake in the whole state. You have Qwest and Safeco Fields, home to the Seattle Seahawks and Mariners, respectively. Mountains Baker, Rainier, and the Olympics look as if they are just beyond the city, though are many miles away. It's awesome.

"Remember all the time we spent at Point Defiance?" I ask.

"Of course, us and Jake, going to the zoo, hanging out at the beach."

"I loved pushing Jake in the water. He'd get so pissed!"

"Well, the water was freezing. Do you remember the Leather Man?"

"Yeah. That old guy that used to lie on the beach every day? I haven't thought about him in years."

"I hear he went there every single day. He would swim then lie on the beach. All year round."

"No wonder his skin looked like an elephant's ass."

"Remember I snuck up on him one day while he was sleeping, just so I could touch his skin and see what it felt like," Kaylee says.

"Yeah, you said . . . what was it? It felt like what an armadillo looks like, or something crazy like that."

"Well, it did," Kaylee squeals.

I take a bunch of pictures of Kaylee. She makes a different goofy face with each push of the button. She grabs the camera from my hands and starts photographing me. I'm a tad bit shyer in front of the camera than Kaylee. Most of the pictures are of me with my hands in front of my face, hiding. Then we take a self-portrait, Seattle looming in the background. We continue to reminisce as night falls. The Seattle skyline lights up, surrounding us in an endless sea of stars.

I eat slowly, savoring every bite, not only because the food is delicious-mouth-watery-goodness, but also because I'm here with Kaylee and I don't want it to end. This is as much a part of my plans as any of the rest, a first date with her, a real date, not a hanging out with friends, watching movies, goofing around date. It's the right time to tell her how I feel, in the dimly lit restaurant, the twinkling Seattle skyline just outside the window.

"Kaylee," I begin.

"Yeah," she says. She looks beautiful in this light.

My tongue twists, and suddenly I can't go any further. I just stare at her stupidly, unable to think, unable to breathe.

"What is it, Austin?" Kaylee asks. "Are you okay? Oh my God, are you choking?" She rushes over, slaps me on the back to dislodge anything that might be stuck in my throat. Of course, the only things stuck are my words.

I feel like a moron. Finally, my tongue moves again, but not in the direction I intend. "I'm okay. Ready to go?" Such an idiot.

"Sure," she says. I think maybe I see disappointment in her eyes, but then I decide it's wishful thinking. I ask for the bill and fake death when it arrives. Kaylee tries to give me a stern look, but ends up in a fit of giggles. I leave a huge tip. It's well worth it, to have had this night, to have shared it with Kaylee. We have our waiter take our picture before we leave. We enjoy the ride back down to the safety of the hard concrete below, then head back to Tacoma.

chapter ten

I crash in the car, as we drive back across town, dead from the busy day. I wake to Kaylee's voice saying sweetly, "We're here." I scan my surroundings blearily, blinking to clear my vision.

"No, no, no. Not here, not yet," I say, realizing we're sitting in front of my house.

"But you're exhausted. It's been a really, really long day. I'm kind of tired myself, you know."

"I know, but I'm not. We're not done yet."

"Not done?" Kaylee asks, confused. "What could you possibly want to do now?"

"It's still early, right? What time?"

Kaylee pulls her cell phone out of her purse and checks the time. "Nine. It's nine o'clock."

"Yes, nine! It's still early. The evening's just starting."

She rolls her eyes and asks, "So where do you want to go, then?"

"Kyle's."

"Kyle's." She was getting into the habit of repeating every destination just after I announce it.

"Yes," I answer.

She stares at me for a moment with cynical eyes.

"No."

"Yes."

"No. Get out."

"Get out? You can't tell me to get out. Besides, if I do, I'm just going to find a ride from someone else, or walk, and then you'll be worried. You wouldn't be able to handle it."

"Forget what I said before about you being crazy," she says. "You're just being stupid now."

"Kaylee," I say, putting my hand on her arm. She jerks away from my touch. "Come on, Kaylee." I give her my best puppy-dog eyes. She can never resist my puppy-dog eyes.

"Austin Parker, you're a fucking whack job," she says. We sit quietly for a moment; I break the silence by laughing. I can't help it. She's right; I feel like a whack job. She looks over, begins to laugh with me, and pulls away from the curb, shaking her head. We head to Kyle's house.

"Justin, Trevor, Suz, and Steph are meeting us there," I inform Kaylee as we approach Kyle's neighborhood, one with big houses, and large trees, and a great stone sign informing us that we're entering Firwood.

"Suz? Why Suz? I hate Suz. Her name isn't even Susan, or

Suzanne, or anything that has to do with her stupid nickname. Her name's Bridgett."

"She doesn't like Bridgett, and come on. You hate her? She's not that bad."

"Okay, I strongly dislike her. Is that better?" she asks.

"I guess," I say, chuckling. "You should really give her a chance."

"She's annoying," Kaylee says.

"No, she just tries too hard. I bet if you reached out to her, she would mellow out."

"I don't want to reach out to her."

"Everyone needs a lifeline once in a while. Why don't you be hers? For me?"

"Lifeline? What is this? *Who Wants to Be a Millionaire?*" She looks at me with an expression of both irritation and admiration. "That's not fair," she says, now pulling onto Kyle's street.

"What's not fair?" I ask.

"You know I'd do anything for you. Now I have to make nice with Suz. Be her *lifeline*," she says, her voice thick with sarcasm. I laugh as we look for a place to park.

Cars are bumper to bumper along the curb, and we have to park a couple blocks away. We can hear the noise, the voices, the music, all the way from our parking spot, the sign of a good party already in progress. We pass our peers, acquaintances, and friends, hanging out at their cars or leaning on trees, as we walk up the street to the party.

Some people whisper as we pass, some wave, some call out to us. I know they must be surprised we're here, since Kaylee and I aren't a part of the regular party crowd. When we get to the front door, Kyle's best friend, Tim, a badass linebacker for the football team, holds out his hand and without looking up says, "Five bucks cover."

I begin to reach for my wallet when Tim looks up. He hesitates; I'm sure because it's me, here, at a party. "You drink for free, Tex." I remember the first time he called me Tex, how I was surprised he knew where Austin is on a map. He's not the sharpest tool in the shed, though he can be a real tool sometimes.

"What about Kaylee?" I ask.

He sizes her up, checks her out. She fidgets and quickly says, "I'm driving—I won't be drinking," seemingly if for no other reason than to end his full body scan.

"Don't matter none. The cute girls drink for free anyway."

Utterly offended, Kaylee asks, "And what about the not-so-cute girls?"

"Five bucks," Tim answers.

"That's so wrong," Kaylee says.

"We don't care if the ugly ones get drunk, just the cute ones."

Kaylee shakes her head and mutters, "Asshole," under her breath. She shoots me a dirty look, as if all of us guys think under some kind of collective mind or something. I shrug.

Tim stamps our hands so we can drink if we want. As we pass, I see him staring at Kaylee's ass out of the corner of my eye. I get pissed, jealous, just a little, but who can blame him, really? She's gorgeous.

We enter the house, smoky, noisy, and crowded, and are received with more whispering, more waving, more greetings. We work our way through the living room, the hallway, to the kitchen where the keg sits. Kyle's there, master of the tap, pouring beer after beer to what appears to be already drunk teens. I hope Kyle has gathered car keys, but I'm sadly sure he hasn't.

When I reach the keg, Kyle sets the tap down and throws his arms around me. "Austin! What up, man? So glad you showed." Kyle, another massive football player, a tight end to be exact, obviously does not know his own strength, as he has just nearly crushed me to death.

"Kyle," I choke, patting his back.

"Oh, sorry, little dude. Are you okay?" Kyle often calls me little dude even though I'm nearly six foot two. Of course, at six foot six, he still towers over me, so I suppose to him the name is fitting.

When I'm finally able to breathe again, I cough out, "Yeah, fine."

Kyle and I aren't what I'd call good friends, more like two people linked together through our parents, who are friends. We like each other just fine, but I'm sure intoxication rather than friendship brought about the hug.

"Want a beer?" Kyle asks.

"Sure," I say.

Kaylee leans in close and whispers in my ear, "I don't like this, Austin. Not at all."

I lean back and whisper, "It's okay, really," trying to reassure her, but know I'm failing miserably.

Kyle writes my name on the cup with a Sharpie and gives me a perfect pour. As the beer fills my cup I ask, "So, your parents out of town?"

"Yeah. They're at one of those lawyer conventions. This one's in Maui."

"Nice," I reply.

He hands over the beer and turns to Kaylee. "One for the lady?"

"No thanks, I'm driving."

"One won't kill you," Kyle says.

"Yeah, it just might," Kaylee answers, annoyed. We head outside to the patio.

"Hi, Austin," I hear from my right. I turn to find Scott McPhee. He was a senior when I was a freshman. We played soccer together. He had everything going for him, a beautiful girlfriend, and a full ride to the University of Portland. Something happened to him, though I don't know what. He lost it. Went down a rough road. Now he's working at Frisko Freeze, flippin' burgers and drinking himself to death.

"Hey, Scott. What's up?"

"The usual."

Kaylee and I continue to a lounge chair by the pool. Not too many people have pools out here in the Pacific Northwest, considering July and August are the only good swimming months and those are sketchy at best. I guess if you're rich enough, which Kyle's parents are, his dad a personal trainer and his mom a lawyer, it's just one more notch in your belt.

I sip the beer slowly and it warms me quickly. I'm getting buzzed fast.

"Austin, what are we doing here?" Kaylee asks me, obviously more than a bit pissed.

"It's just part of the process, the natural order of things."

My buzz tells me I sound profound, philosophical even. In reality, I sound like a dick.

"The natural order? A kegger? You have to experience a kegger? We're not kegger people, Austin. We're music and movie and art people. We're sports people. But we're definitely not kegger people."

I laugh; she gets more irritated. I ask her to get me another beer. She gets really irritated. She swipes the cup from my hand and heads back inside.

While Kaylee is grabbing me another beer, people approach, say hi, slap me on the back, ask how I'm doing. Kyle, taking a break from being tap master, comes around socializing; he takes a seat next to me, hands me another beer.

"So how're you doing, Austin? Really?"

"As good as I'll ever be."

"That's great. Say, you and, um, what's her name?"

"Kaylee," I answer.

"Yeah, Kaylee. Are you guys, you know?" He gestures by creating a hole with one hand and inserting the index finger of the other.

"Nah, it's not like that. We're just friends," I say, a little pissed at his crudeness. Even if we were dating, I would never look at her that way, like a piece of meat.

"That's too bad. She's pretty hot."

I feel myself getting drunker, being the amateur drinker I am. My tongue ties; my speech slurs just a little. "Yeah, she's beautiful."

"Ah, you like her," Kyle says, winking.

"No," I say. "I love her."

"You should tell her, you know."

"Yeah, I know." Kyle pats me on the shoulder and gets up to leave. I stop him. "Hey, Kyle?"

"Yeah, little dude," he says.

"This drinking thing, it's not so great."

Kyle laughs. "You seem to be having fun."

"I don't know; it's kind of a waste of time, isn't it."

Kyle sits back down and says, "Sometimes I get so worked up, so jacked, I just need to relax. Drinking helps me relax, you know?"

"There are other ways to relax," I say.

"What is this, some kind of intervention?"

"No, nothing like that . . . I just passed Scott McPhee. I just don't want to see you end up like that."

Kyle looks back toward Scott. "Yeah, he looks like shit, huh?"

"Yeah."

"That sucks," he says, then gives me a weird look. "Hey, Austin, you might want to slow down. You're looking a little pasty there, dude." He gets up. I look down at the beer he has just given me, and it's already halfway gone.

"One more thing," I say.

"What's that?"

"Are you gonna be home tomorrow?"

"Nah. I've got some shit to do. I won't be home until the afternoon. We can hang out some other time, if you want."

"Sure, sounds great," I say, although hanging out with him isn't what I have in mind. I have other plans that involve him not being home.

Out of nowhere, we hear, "Bitch!" Turning toward the noise, I see Ben and Juliana on the other side of the pool.

Though I can't hear what she says, I can tell she's pleading with him. "Shut up!" he yells.

I put my beer down on the ground and stand up. "What are you doing, little dude?" Kyle asks.

"He shouldn't talk to her like that," I answer, heading toward them. Kyle jumps up after me.

"This is not a good idea, Austin. He'll tear you apart."

"You'll stop him, won't you?" I smile and pat Kyle's huge shoulder. He just shakes his head as he follows.

As we're approaching, Ben sees us and says, "What do you want?"

"Leave her alone, Ben," I say.

"Mind your own business," he says. I look at Juliana; she's crying. She shakes her head at me to stop, but I can't. The beer has given me courage I would probably lack if sober.

I look back to Ben. "She doesn't deserve that."

"What do you know about what she deserves? Oh, that's right, because word has it you paid her a visit today. What were you doing at my girlfriend's house, Austin? Getting some sloppy seconds?" He moves in closer, shoves a finger in my chest.

"No, we were talking. And don't touch me."

"Get your own girl, retard," he says, once again poking me.

Juliana touches his arm, asks him to stop. He backhands her, sends her crashing into a chair and onto the ground. I lunge at him but am caught by one of Kyle's muscular arms. "I got this," he says. He puts an arm around Ben's shoulder and walks him straight into the house and, I'm hoping, out the front door.

I offer Juliana a hand up. "Are you okay?" I ask.

"You shouldn't have done that. You probably just made it worse."

"I don't know. Maybe Kyle can talk some sense into him."

"Or beat it into him," she says simply. I think that's not

such a bad idea. "You really should mind your own business," she says, then grabs a friend and turns to go.

I should leave it at that, but I can't help myself. I shout at her, "Should I? Really? Should I mind my own business? I'm just trying to help, to show you that you're worth something. You deserve better than to be treated like a punching bag. Life is too short to waste time with people like Ben, Juliana." My diatribe falls on deaf ears. She never stops, never turns back around. She just leaves me standing there. Epic fail.

I walk back to my chair full of self-loathing, but my mood immediately adjusts when I hear someone yell, "Austin!" My friends have arrived: Justin, his girlfriend, Stephanie, and Trevor and Suz.

"Austin, what's up?" Justin greets me with a fist bump. Justin, Jake, and I all played soccer together since like seventh grade. Jake was the keeper, Justin a midfielder, and I played forward. I haven't been able to play the last two years, though. When all three of us were on the field, there was no stopping us. I had speed and skills, Justin had a sick passing foot, and you couldn't get a shot past Jake. We had an undefeated season a couple years ago. It came down to a penalty kick. Jake leapt into the air and batted it down—it was sweet. I'll never forget it.

I've known both Justin and Steph since middle school. Steph was always hanging out at our soccer practices and games, like a soccer groupie. I still don't know if she actually likes soccer or just soccer players. Maybe it's a little of both. She dated Jake first, for about six months in the seventh grade, until she realized that Jake's skateboard was more important to him than anything else, including her. She and Justin have been together for three years now, on and off. They're together, they fight, they break up, they make up—it's a cycle. Right now they're in the makeup stage.

"Just kickin' back, having some brews. Man, what's up with the soccer team this year?"

Justin gets a pained look on his face. "I know, we suck. It's not the same without you on the pitch. No way Dylan can take your place."

"I wish I could still play. That totally blows," I say.

"Well, what doesn't kill you only makes you stronger, right?" Justin says, laughing.

"Nah, sometimes it just kills you," I say. Suz gasps, and everyone else gets quiet. I laugh. "Just a joke, people."

"Real fucking profound, Austin," Justin says.

"That wasn't funny," Steph adds.

"It's not supposed to be funny, Steph," I say harshly, though I think it's more the alcohol talking than me. I stand up and knock my beer over. "It's just true. Sometimes we don't get stronger. We just die, slowly, until we're nothing but a pile of bones waiting to be ground to ash and blown away in the wind. And then we won't even be a memory; we'll just be a blip of something that once was." I feel out of control as the words spill out of me as my beer has spilled out over the concrete patio.

"Not if you make your mark, man," Justin says.

"Make my mark? How the fuck am I supposed to make my mark, Justin? I'm already dying. We're all dying; we just don't know how and when it will happen. Well, at least, the lucky ones don't." Philosophical yes, but also drunk off my ass.

"Austin, maybe you should stop drinking," Stephanie says. She's worried. A sweet girl, but at the moment her concern is pissing me off.

"That's what Kaylee would say," I answer.

"Well, maybe you should think about it, then. Kaylee really cares about you," Steph says.

"Kaylee doesn't know everything," Suz adds.

"Yeah, what Suz said," I say.

"Is that right?" Kaylee has snuck up behind me, beer in hand.

"I'm just saying," Suz backpedals, "you're not like the

beer police or an alcohol expert or anything. I think if Austin wants to have a beer, he should be able to."

"Well, this," Kaylee says as she holds my cup up and jiggles it around, sloshing beer to the ground, "is his second."

I hold up three fingers and say, "Third." I grab the cup from Kaylee's hand. She glares at me and turns her attention back to Suz.

"Just how many do you think he should be able to have?"

"As many as he wants," Suz says. She turns to me and smiles in triumph. She's cute, that's for sure—a tiny little thing, with dark hair and big brown eyes—but she's no Kaylee. Although she's a bit high maintenance, her friendship is a necessity. She became part of our little group when Trevor did. They're twins, and very much inseparable. They look exactly alike but are different in every other way. Where Trevor is shy, Suz is outgoing, on the verge of obnoxious. Where Trevor is reserved, she's an open book. Where Trevor is highly intelligent, Suz is a bit of an airhead, although I wouldn't doubt if that was more for show than an actual lack of intelligence.

I smile at her.

I look over and see that Trevor is the only one in the bunch without a beer. "Aren't you going to have one?" I ask him.

"Nope. I'm driving."

"Good man," I say, offering a salute. Trevor and I didn't

really start hanging out until we found ourselves waiting in the same line for Shins tickets. Before that, he'd always seemed like a snob. He's just incredibly shy. Looking at us, you would never guess that we're friends. I mean, I'm tall, athletic, strong—at least, I used to be. Trevor looks kind of emo, rail thin, dark hair, guyliner, wears black all the time. Our taste in music brought us together, but we've found some other stuff in common too.

Kaylee takes the seat next to me, crosses her arms over her chest, and gives me the silent treatment. I am beyond caring. I drink my beer, this time a bit quicker. I stumble in to get another. Kaylee follows. She pulls me by the coat, around the corner of the house. "What the hell are you doing, Austin?"

"I'm enjoying one of the very important teenage rituals, getting drunk." I've lost control of my tongue and the words come out slurred. I wonder if Kaylee even understands me.

"This is stupid." Yep. She understands me. "And the entire house and most of north side could hear your little rant. What the hell was that all about?"

"You don't get it! None of you. How can you?" I don't want to, but I cry; I can't help it.

"I know that you're going through some hard times right now, Austin," Kaylee says. "But it's going to get better."

"Don't say that. It's not going to get better."

"You don't know that," Kaylee says. She tries to reassure me, but she can't. It's too late.

"Yes, I do." I look at her and see that she's terrified, maybe even more than I am. I've done enough damage. "I'm going to get my beer. Go back to the party. I'll be right there."

"Are you sure, Austin?"

"Yeah, go. I'm right behind you."

I calm down and am about to turn the corner when I hear Steph's and Justin's voices. They're fighting, as usual.

"What about the homecoming dance?" I hear Steph say.

"You've got to be kidding me," Justin says. "I was sick, puking my guts out. What did you expect me to do?"

"I don't know. But by the time you called, everyone had already left. I couldn't get a ride. I had to stay home."

"Oh, yeah, well, what about the time I caught you making out with Bobby Meyers, huh?" Justin says.

"I didn't make out with him. He kissed me. I told you that. He cornered me against the wall. I couldn't get away. Jesus, I was happy to see you. I thought he was going to rape me."

"How did he get you cornered, huh?" Justin asks.

"I don't know, maybe because he caught me off-guard and he's about a foot taller and a hundred pounds heavier than me," Steph says. "And who are you to talk? Right after that you kissed Keisha Washington."

"I was pissed at you for kissing Bobby Meyers, duh, Steph," Justin says.

I think about stepping in, but I really don't care. Their problems are nothing compared to mine. I walk around the corner past them, don't stop, don't talk, just keep walking. By the time I'm back outside, they're making out. I sit back down next to Kaylee and drink my beer. She puts a hand on my knee and smiles. I melt. Then, I get right back into the conversation and chat about old times with my friends. I have to concentrate to keep my tongue from tripping over itself.

"Austin, remember that Death Cab concert you and I went to?" Suz asks. "You know, the one when Trev got sick and couldn't go with you? That was so fun!" she gushes.

Kaylee leans in, whispers, "You know she likes you, right? It's so obvious, the way she hangs on your every word and gazes at you endlessly. And seriously, I think she's trying to make me jealous."

"Nah, she doesn't like me. We're just friends," I respond, leaning in, almost falling in her lap. Then I ask, "Are you?"

"Am I what?"

"Jealoush." The beer is forcing me to add the *sh* sound to

the beginning and end of many of my words. Amazing, the effect of alcohol on the tongue.

"Well, of course I'm not jealous. That's stupid." She's defensive, but maintains her whisper. "What do I have to be jealous of? It's not like you and I are dating or something."

"Nah, I guesh not," I say.

"I mean, we're just friends, right?"

"Yep. Sure," I answer, wishing I were wrong.

I remember I have something to ask Trevor. "Hey, Trevor!" I shout, the beer making me speak louder than I should.

"What's up, Austin?"

"Are you gonna be home tomorrow?"

"Yeah, I'll be home."

"Good, I'm gonna come over. I've got shomething I want to talk to you about."

"Okay," he responds, sounding confused.

Kaylee shoots me a puzzled look. I shrug her off.

I'm warm, tired, and drunk, so drunk I'm starting to feel sick. It's time to go. "I'm ready," I inform Kaylee.

"It's about time," she says. She snatches her purse and gets ready to leave.

I begin to get up, but my legs give out from under me. Kaylee lunges to catch me, and together we fall down on the lounge chair, face-to-face, her on top of me. I hear giggling, but ignore it. Kaylee and I stare into each other's eyes for a moment. I've never been so close to those eyes. For the first time I notice flecks of green swimming among the blue, like little fish in a deep lake.

Her beauty astounds me. It's time. It's the right time. I open my mouth to speak. "Kaylee," I say, but she stops me, pressing her index and middle fingers gently to my lips.

"Shhh. You're drunk," she says.

"But, Kaylee, I—" I start again.

She presses her fingers harder, but gentle still, down on my lips. "Austin, you're drunk. Whatever you need to say can wait until tomorrow. Please, let's just go."

I nod and she removes her fingers from my mouth. Though totally wasted, I understand. Although I want to, I shouldn't tell her like this, drunk, nearly passed out. The beer would make it so much easier, but it wouldn't be right, the way it should be remembered. She would wonder if I'd really meant it or if the beer were talking.

She offers me a hand, pulls me from the lounge chair, and motions for Kyle to help. Kyle runs over, lifts me up, and throws me over his shoulder. I'm too drunk to be embarrassed.

"Hi, Kyle," I say.

"Hey, little dude. You okay?"

"I'm great." I smile as only an incredibly sloshed virgin drinker can.

He carries me through the house and out the front door, and hauls me down the two blocks to the car, Kaylee following. She unlocks and opens the passenger door and Kyle slides and buckles me in, shutting the door behind me. I can hear Kyle ask Kaylee if I'm going to be okay. Kaylee says nothing. I assume she has nodded or shrugged.

Kaylee comes around the driver's side, gets in, and starts up Candy. I look over at her; I can tell she's pissed. "Kaylee," I say.

She whips her head around like something from *The Exorcist,* glares at me, and interrupts, loudly, "Listen, Austin. I do not want you to say a goddamn thing, okay?"

"But Kaylee," I say.

"Not a thing, Austin. I mean it. You might say something you'll regret later. You're shitfaced, you're tired, and your brain has probably turned to mush. Final warning."

"Kaylee," I continue.

"No, Austin," she says.

"Kaylee, I'm sorry." And then I puke. All over the front of me, all over the dash, all over everything.

"Jesus," she mutters under her breath, rolling down her

window to let the stench escape into the night air. Then she says, "Austin, I appreciate what you're trying to do here, really, I do, but I think you're in over your head." She's starting to sound like my mother. I stop listening, lay my head back, and let sleep take over.

I don't remember getting home, into my house, out of my puke-covered clothes, into my bed. All I remember is waking to the feeling of a vise strapped to my head, crushing it slowly until it fractures.

day two . . .

chapter eleven

I sleep in later than I want, but it's still early, and I have a lot more to do before the end of the weekend. It hurts to move, but I force myself out of bed. In the bathroom, I gaze into my reflection, wondering if this is how I'll look when I'm dead. I feel like I already am. I'm sure dead people don't have blood-shot eyes. I have bloodshot eyes, and they hurt, but not as bad as my head. I promise myself never to drink again.

I reach into the medicine cabinet, grab a couple of Tyle-nol, and take the stairs slowly, my head pounding with every step. I enter the kitchen and sit at the table, placing the pills carefully down beside me.

"You got in late," Mom says. She's cooking something that on a normal day probably smells good. This morning it stinks, making me want to barf.

"Did I?" I ask. Big mistake. My mom throws a glare my direction. Here it comes. I feel it.

"You know, Austin—?" Yes, I knew it. "I don't know ex-actly what you were out doing all day yesterday and last night, but I hope whatever it was was worth it and not too self-destructive."

"Did you put me to bed?" I ask, deciding to ignore her lecture.

She lets out a heavy sigh and answers, "No, I was in bed myself when you got home." Just what I feared: Kaylee stripped my drunk ass out of my puke-covered clothes and put me to bed. I hope I hadn't said or done anything stupid, or pissed her off. I can't remember much after throwing up all over her car.

"You want something to go with those?" my mom says. She gestures to the Tylenol sitting on the table.

"OJ," I answer.

She pours a tall glass and sets it down in front of me. "You hungry?"

"Definitely not," I answer, my stomach churning with nausea.

"You shouldn't go without breakfast."

"A dry piece of toast then," I concede.

I eat the toast and head back up to my room. As I'm leaving Mom asks, "So what's on the schedule for today?"

"Same as yesterday," I answer, not looking in her direction purposely. I'm not in the mood for the cynical expression I know she's giving me. She doesn't stop me, which to me is a sign of resignation. I start to feel guilty. I turn back around. "Love you, Mom."

"Love you too, kiddo," she says, not looking up from the dishes.

I continue up the stairs to my room and lie back on my bed, wondering what I would feel like if I hadn't thrown up. When the Tylenol kicks in, I shower and begin to dress. My mother calls up.

"Austin! I'm going to the store. You need anything?"

"No!" I shout back.

"Oh, and you have company!"

"Be right down!" I answer. Kaylee. I must not have done too much damage to our relationship. I finish dressing: flannel shirt, shorts, wool socks, hiking boots. I double-check myself in the mirror and head downstairs.

Instead of Kaylee, Allie is sitting on my living room couch.

"Allie?"

"Hi, Austin."

I sit down beside her. "What's up?"

She stands, paces, wrings her hands. Nervous. "Well, I was thinking." She takes a deep breath. "I appreciate you coming over yesterday, letting me vent and everything. I thought maybe you would want me to return the favor."

"It wasn't a favor, Allie. You don't need to pay me back. I just want to help. I want to know that you're okay."

"I know. I just thought I could do something for you in return," she says, approaching, kneeling, leaning on my thighs.

"What, Allie? What do you want to do for me?"

"What do I want to do for you?" she says, mostly to herself. "Well, it's more like something I want to give you."

"What's that?"

"Me."

"What are you talking about?"

"Well, you're a virgin, right?" she asks, now starting to caress my legs.

"Allie, no."

"I know you are. So, I just thought maybe you would like to, you know, know what you're doing, just in case you and Kaylee decide . . ." Her voice drops away.

"No."

"Yes," she says, getting quietly hysterical. "In case it happens for you and Kaylee, then it won't be weird, ya know? You'll know what to do, how to do it. We don't have to do it now. We can meet somewhere, or get a hotel room. Or you could come to my house. My parents are never home anyway."

I stand up, grab her hands, fix my eyes on her black-eyeliner-laden ones. She's tearing up, wounded, offended in some way. I need to be careful with her.

"Allie, listen. You're great, really. I don't want this from you, or for you. I came to see you because I missed you and hoped to help you, not as a favor. Helping you wasn't my only reason for visiting. I was being selfish. I'm searching for meaning, Allie, even if it's just a shred, before it's too late. Sex is the furthest thing from my mind right now, even with Kaylee."

"Really?" She looks at me achingly, but thoughtfully. "Meaning, huh? Maybe it's time I found some meaning too? Before it's too late?"

"I think that's a good idea," I say.

She heads to the front door; I follow. She stops, reaches up, touches my face, then smiles and says, "You know you're cute, right?"

I smile back. "Really?"

"Yes, really. I just thought you should know."

"Thank you." I grab her hand from my face, kiss her palm, and hold her hand as she heads out the door. I watch as she walks down the sidewalk. Suddenly I see something very different about her, something positive, something like confidence. I start to feel better about my visit with her. I think she'll be okay.

chapter twelve

I gather my stuff and head out, thinking the fresh air will relieve what's left of my hangover. The sky's a strange shade of gray this morning, almost a gray yellow, as if the sun is there just beyond the clouds, desperately trying to break through. I automatically move in the direction of Kaylee's house. It's where I need to be anyway. I ring the bell, wait. Ring the bell again. Kaylee finally answers, looking really pissed, I might add.

"What are you supposed to be? The Brawny paper towel guy?" she says eyeballing my outfit. "I didn't figure you'd be up yet." Her delivery stings. I flinch.

"You busy?" I ask, hoping she says no. Once again, she's a big part of my plans for the day.

"I'm getting ready for work, duh," she answers, gesturing to her coffee shop black. Her tone cuts to my very core.

"Call in sick," I say.

"No," she says, thrusting the blade deeper.

"Please," I plead. Something in my voice or perhaps my

manner causes her to soften. Her attitude changes instantly from anger to compassion, yet she doesn't budge.

"I can't, Austin. I need the money."

"I'll pay your wages today if you call in sick," I offer.

"Austin, I'm not for sale," she says, though I see she's starting to waver. Her eyes move, roll around. She's thinking.

"I'll buy you breakfast." She doesn't budge.

I fold my hands as in prayer, get down on my knees, put on my best puppy-dog face, and repeat, "Please."

She shakes her head. I bow down, as if to a goddess, and say, "I'm not worthy, I'm not worthy." I give her a sideways glance. She tries not to laugh.

She gives me a stern glare behind the smirk. "Fine, but no more keggers."

"Deal," I say, happily relieved.

Kaylee calls in sick. "I'll go change," she says.

"Dress warm. Oh, and you'll need your hiking boots," I tell her.

"Great," she says.

As I wait, Mrs. Davis enters from the kitchen. "Are you corrupting my daughter, Austin? I thought she was just getting ready for work," she says.

"Sorry, Mrs. Davis. I really need her to drive me around again today. You're not mad, are you?"

"How could anyone get mad at you? She said you guys

went to Seattle yesterday?" When she says this she gets a sad look on her face.

I mentioned that two bad things happened in sixth grade. The first was when Kaylee's dad died. It was a horrible car crash. I remember Kaylee not showing up for school. In second period, our teacher told us that her dad had died. I tried to call her all afternoon, but no one answered the phone. She called me back the next day, wanted to go for a walk, to get out of the house, to get away from the tears, the pain.

She seemed so fragile—trembling, crying, not sure what to do with herself. I didn't know what to do either. I put an arm around her awkwardly as we walked. I listened, gave her a shoulder. It was hard to see her like that, but man, did I want to kiss her. I was mad at myself for thinking that right then, when she was so sad.

Mrs. Davis was like a rock after the death. I'm sure she did it for her girls. Everyone was amazed that she could be so strong through such a hard time. I knew she was dying inside. I saw it.

I came over one day, unannounced, just before the funeral. My mom had made a chicken and noodle casserole. I brought it over. The front door was open, so I let myself in, as I had so many times before. I headed toward the kitchen. There she sat, alone at the dining room table, head in her hands. She sobbed so deep and so violently, it seemed she couldn't breathe. I didn't know what to do. As quietly as I could, I set the casserole dish down on the coffee table in the living room. Then I snuck back out of the house. She stayed strong for those girls, but there was no one there to be strong for her. I'm sure she felt alone. Anyway, that's the reason I can't call her anything but Mrs. Davis. I don't believe I've earned that right.

When Kaylee comes down the stairs, we quickly pack a backpack with a couple snacks, waters, and first-aid supplies, and we're climbing into the Mustang ten minutes later.

"Do you think Candy's up for the drive?" I ask, patting the car's dash.

"Crap."

"What?"

"She still smells like Puke de Austin."

"Funny," I say. She gives me a dirty look, letting me know she's not exactly joking. The car does smell a little bit funky.

"Plus, her name isn't Candy anymore," Kaylee says.

"Oh, did you change her name to Apple, like I suggested?"

"No, I still think that's a stupid name. Her name is Scarlet now."

"Scarlet? Sounds like a slut," I joke.

"You shouldn't say things like that in front of her, Austin. She's still pissed at you for throwing up all over her last night. I was up an extra hour cleaning her out and dousing her with Lysol to get rid of the stench. Take a whiff," she says, sniffing deeply. "She still reeks. That's why I changed the name. A car stinking of beer vomit can't possibly be named Candy, now can it?"

"But a car stinking of beer vomit can be named Scarlet?"

"You're not winning any points here, Austin," Kaylee says.

I pet the dash as if it's a kitten on my lap. "I'm sorry, Scarlet. Believe me, it won't happen again." Then, less mockingly: "I'm sorry to you too, Kaylee."

"Whatever," she replies. "I could have used your help last night, Paper Towel Boy."

"Yeah, funny. Can we go now?" I ask.

"Where're we headed?"

"Mount Rainier."

"Well, that explains the logger look." Despite the comment, her mood changes. "I love hiking."

"We're only going a couple miles. I want to see something beautiful today," I say.

"Uh, hello?" Kaylee says, pointing to herself.

I roll my eyes. She's right, though. I can't think of anything more beautiful than her.

Kaylee turns to me with troubled eyes. "Are you sure you're up for that today? We had a long day yesterday, and I *know* you had a rough night last night. You've got to be hurtin'," she says.

"I'll work through the pain, and yeah, about that, thanks for, um, putting me to bed and stuff. I appreciate it," I tell her, head hung low. I feel my cheeks blush. Kaylee smiles a goofy smile, shakes her head, and turns her attention back to the road.

"Before we go to Rainier, two quick pit stops," I tell her.

"Oh, yeah. To where?"

"Micky D's, but first Kyle's."

"Kyle's? Is he coming with us?" Kaylee asks.

"No. He's not home," I answer.

She eyes me suspiciously. "Then why are we going there?"

"Just for a quick dip."

"Here we go again," Kaylee says driving to Kyle's house.

We park down the street just as we had the night before, not for lack of parking, but for discretion. If you're going to break into someone's backyard, it's not a good idea to park right in the driveway. We slip down the street, hiding behind bushes and trees as we go, tiptoeing, as if secret agents. We sneak to the side of Kyle's house.

It's still trashed from last night's festivities—cups, bottles, cans, and cigarette butts litter the yard and street. Kyle obviously did not have time to clean before heading out this morning.

A locked six-foot fence surrounds the pool. We have to scale it, which is not an easy task. Kaylee helps me up and over first, she being the stronger of the two of us. She follows, nearly falling on top of me as she climbs over. Lucky for me she hits a rosebush instead.

"Ouch," she cries.

"Shhh."

She whispers, "Austin, I would normally say this is one of the dumbest ideas you've ever had, but after yesterday, I guess it only makes the top twenty."

"Nice, Kaylee, nice."

"So what's with the secret swim? Why couldn't you just come over when Kyle was home?"

"Because I want to do something I've never done before. I want to skinny-dip."

"Skinny-dip?"

"Yes, and I don't want to do it with Kyle."

"You don't think I'm going to do it with you, do you?"

"That's not what I said."

"Are you sure he's not home?"

"Yes."

"Okay, have at it. I'll just go sit in that lounge chair over there, not watching."

"Fine, but keep a lookout. Just in case." I begin stripping my clothes off, the cold wind stinging every inch of my bare skin, causing an outbreak of goose bumps. I slide into the pool slowly, not wanting to alert the neighbors by splashing around loudly. The water feels like icicles against my skin. Kaylee's sitting in a lounge chair with her back to me. "I'm in. You can turn around now," I tell her.

She turns, leans back on the chair, watches me swim. God, I'd love nothing more than to see her in this pool, naked, swimming with me. The thought excites me, affects my body in ways that make me braver than usual. "You want to come in with me?"

"No thanks."

"Why not?"

"First of all, it looks like it's colder than shit. Second of all, that would mean me getting naked. Uh-uh."

"Come on. I've seen a naked girl before. You've seen one, you've seen them all."

"Right. What naked girls have you seen? The ones in *Playboy*?"

"Juliana."

"Juliana? But I thought—"

"Just because we never had sex doesn't mean we didn't get naked."

"Oh." She has a strange look on her face. It's difficult to read.

"And you've seen naked guys before." It's no secret between us that Kaylee has had sexual relationships. There's been two to be exact, so she's not a virgin like I am. She doesn't share much about those relationships—they weren't very good I guess—but she has shared that there was sex involved.

"Yeah, and you know I love it when you bring that up."

"Tell me about them."

"Why? They're in the past."

"Because I'm curious. Because normally we tell each other everything, and you've never really talked about them."

"Fine. The first was Brian. A boy whose family's lake place was next to my grandparents'. You know, I've gone there for years during the summers. Brian was always there, ever since I was about six years old. He was three years older than me. Well, the summer I was thirteen, we started holding hands, kissing, small stuff like that. The next summer it got a little steamier. He'd slip his hand up my shirt, down my pants—things just progressed."

Listening to her talk about it makes me imagine doing those things to her, and I feel myself harden. I'm relieved I'm in the pool where she can't see and where the cold water easily fixes the problem.

"The last weekend of the summer, we snuck out after everyone had gone to bed, went down to the lake, and lay in the sand. He was more aggressive than usual that night; I didn't fight it. In truth I didn't realize what was happening until it was happening. Within minutes we were stripped down and were . . . you know. When it was over, which was pretty quick, I kind of felt this sense of loss. Kind of empty. It's the last time I ever saw him. My grandpa died in the winter, and Grandma had to sell the place. We e-mailed at first, called, but the more time went by, the more sporadic the communications became until they just went away for good."

"What was it like? Your first time, I mean."

"It was almost surreal, like a bad dream. Not a nightmare, just a dream you wished you'd never had. It hurt; there was a lot of blood. But, I think it's almost better to get that first time out of the way with someone you don't really care about, because it's so uncomfortable and not really very fun."

"And what was the other one's name?"

"Jimmy. He was sweet. He worshiped me. I tried for a while with him, just because he was so nice. But something was missing. The butterflies, the heart flutters. I just didn't really feel for him the way I should have."

"Are you sure you don't want to come in, please?"

"Austin, give it up already." She laughs. "I'm not getting in there." I know when I'm defeated.

"I'm getting out. Turn around," I say more sharply than I should, my tone surprising even me. I think listening to her talk about her relationships frustrates me, makes me jealous. They make me wonder what those guys had that she doesn't see in me. The day is just beginning, though; I still have time to open her eyes.

I hear the slider open. "Someone's here," I say a little too loud. I try running out of the pool, which of course feels like slow motion. When I get to the stairs, I jump out, too frantic to care that Kaylee is seeing me in all my glory. She grabs my clothes and starts handing me one piece at a time while we run to the fence. I hastily slip them on.

Kyle says, "What the—?"

Kaylee jumps up and over the fence. I struggle to get up. She is looking up at me from the other side. "Come on, Austin," she mouths, motioning me forward.

Suddenly, I feel a hand on my back. I turn and find Kyle standing there. He nods and smiles. I start to say something, but he presses his finger to his lips as if to say "Shhh." He cradles his hands and gives me a leg up. As I climb over the top, he gives me the thumbs-up, still smiling. I smile back and slide down the other side of the fence.

"Jesus, Austin. I can't believe you didn't get caught," Kaylee says as we run down the street toward her car.

"Yeah, weird."

"I thought you said Kyle wasn't supposed to be home." She's annoyed, I can tell. I just shrug and smile.

chapter thirteen

When we arrive at the mountain, the sun is just starting to poke through the September clouds. We grab our gear out of the trunk of the car and head up the hill.

"Have you ever been here before?" I ask Kaylee.

"Never. You?"

"Tons. I used to go hiking with Mom and Dad before, well, you know." Kaylee looks at me sympathetically. "You're going to love this," I tell her.

This is my favorite hike, surrounded by trees and sky and soil. I've run into squirrels and marmots and even a black bear once. Nature has always been big for me, its raw beauty and magnificence. Sometimes I think about the trees and the mountains and how long they've been here. Much longer than I've been alive, and they'll be here long after I've gone. It makes you realize how small you are in the scheme of things, what little impact you have on the world. It's part of the reason why I'm doing what I'm doing this weekend, to make an impact. To know I might have made a difference, even if it was a small one.

The hike starts straight up but evens out quickly. After walking a quarter mile, we cross a bridge and stop in the middle to admire the scenery, Christine Falls. The water rushes down the rocks and underneath us. I put my pack down and pull out a water and a PowerBar to share. "This is beautiful," Kaylee says.

I want to say *Not as beautiful as you,* but I stop myself, not wanting to sound stupid. Instead, I say, "This is nothing. Come on." We repack our stuff and head farther up the mountain.

Kaylee looks at her surroundings in wonder, like a child first discovering the world around her. This makes me happy; it's what I wanted. I wanted to share this with her, this place that has always been so important to me.

We walk side by side with the falls as it snakes up the mountain. The trail heads away from the water and we weave through the trees, the sound of the falls waxing and waning with every turn. The hike evens out a bit again but soon we're climbing steps made of rocks and tree roots. The farther we go, the steeper the trail gets, and I begin to struggle. Kaylee notices.

"Are you doing okay?" she asks.

"Yep. Couldn't be better." It's only a small lie. I feel okay, just a little tired.

We hike up and down, but mostly up. I'm getting weak; my lungs feel as if they will explode at any moment. The sound of the falling water becomes louder, and a few minutes later we're looking down over a ravine. There's a Y of water falling from two different sources and a tiny, one-rail bridge beneath them. "Wow," Kaylee whispers as she begins her descent into the ravine. I move slowly, as my legs feel like Jell-O and the ground is steep and slippery. I take only three steps before I lose my footing and end up on my ass.

Kaylee turns back, sees me on the ground, and rushes to my aid. "Are you okay? I should have helped you down," she says, offering me a hand up.

"Yeah, I'm fine," I say, though my tailbone throbs in pain. She takes my hand and leads me down the rocks to the bridge. Again we stop in the middle to take in the view. Water shoots down over a cliff and rolls under us.

"This is amazing," Kaylee says.

"It's okay."

She turns to me with a look that says WTF, then says, "Just okay? Why would you climb a mountain for something that's just okay?"

"I mean, it's all right, but it's nothing compared to Comet Falls."

Kaylee gives me a strange look before looking back up to the falling water, then again at me, and says, "This isn't the waterfall?"

"Nope."

"Then what's this?"

"This is a creek."

"A creek? This huge waterfall thingy is just a creek?"

"Yep. Van Trump Creek."

"Well, if this is a creek, I can't wait to see the waterfall."

"Then let's go."

This is where the really hard climbing begins—switchbacks straight up, back and forth. I have to stop often to rest, but Kaylee's patience never wavers. As we climb farther up, the air starts to chill. It's crisp and smells like snow. Kaylee's cute little nose is turning red; I want to kiss it warm. I'd forgotten how cold it gets up here, no matter how hot it is down at the bottom of the trail. The sun is bright, though, and heats the sections of trails not shadowed by the tall fir trees.

We take yet another break—more water, trail mix. I pull a black stocking hat out of the backpack. Kaylee laughs at me. "Brawny turns gangsta," she says.

"You're a goofball."

She's keeping a watchful eye on me, I can tell. "You sure you're up to this?"

"Yes, I'm sure, and it would be silly to turn back now after coming this far."

We're closing in on our destination—I can tell because the temperature has dropped even more, the water's scent carries through the breeze, and the sound of the falls beats in my ears and heart like a bass drum.

"That's loud," Kaylee yells over the noise.

"We're almost there," I yell back. Which is good because I feel like I'm about to collapse.

Kaylee appears awestruck when we finally reach what we came to see, Comet Falls, three hundred and twenty feet of cascading glacier water—in my eyes, one of God's most beautiful works of art. Water rockets off the bluff, crashes into the rocks below, then winds down the mountainside. On a hot day, it's fun to go right down to the base and let the water splash onto your legs. It's too cold for that, so we watch from the rocks, but our faces still get misted. We sit. Kaylee tears up, whether moved by the view or something more, I don't know. She gropes around blindly, aimlessly with her hand, not wanting to take her eyes off the breathtaking scene before her. I take hold, squeeze tight. She moves in closer and lays her head on my shoulder.

"Tell me about your future, Kaylee," I say.

"What do you mean?"

"I want you to tell me what the future holds for you.

What you want to do, what you want to be. Where you picture yourself five years from now, or ten."

She looks at me, says, "I guess it would start with an education. I'm not necessarily talking college, but definitely business courses. You see, I have this crazy idea of owning my own coffee and book bar."

"Why's it so crazy? It sounds perfect for you."

"I don't know. Owning a business seems kind of scary."

"You'll be great at it. A natural. What happens next? Marriage? Family?"

Now she takes her eyes from me, looks down in her lap. "I always imagined marrying an artist, a painter, or an actor—mostly, a writer." My heart begins to ache. "I could work the coffee shop while he sits at his laptop. We'd take breaks together."

"Kids?"

"Yes. Two, doesn't matter boys, girls, one of each, as long as they're healthy. And a cat."

"A cat?"

"Yeah, a tabby."

"Sounds nice."

Her eyes find mine again. "What about you, Austin? What did you imagine your life being like?"

"Maybe going to college on a soccer scholarship while studying English and literature. Marrying the girl of my dreams. She'd be beautiful in every way—heart, mind, and soul. Kids."

"Recite me one of your poems," she says.

"Let me think. Okay, how about this one.

I'm a ghost, but nothing more.
Air and vapor, invisible.
With a heart that beats a rhythm so rare
Only the stars can hear.
And she, of flesh and bone,
Alive, wild, gleaming.
Hovering above I watch her
Gliding, rushing, reeling.
My empty arms reach out for her
To touch, to feel, to know.
Yet I'm a ghost and nothing more.
Air and vapor, invisible."

"It's beautiful, Austin, but tragic at the same time. Is it about the one that got away?"

"More like the one that never was."

We grow silent among the water and the trees and the mountain air, breathing it in, feeling it pulse within us. Then Kaylee says, "Wouldn't it be great if we could just sit here and stay like this forever?"

"Yeah, it would," I answer. "Let's take a picture so we can." I take my camera from the backpack and we take a photo, falls at our back.

"Austin, do you believe in heaven?"

"I have to."

"What do you think it's like? Do you think it's like this?"

"I think heaven is anything you want it to be."

Hungry, I grab another PowerBar and another water and begin to munch. Kaylee's stomach growls, so I hand her a PowerBar as well. I take some more pictures, sneak in a couple candid ones of Kaylee, and shove the camera back in the bag. We make our descent holding hands.

The climb down is much easier, at least for me, using stronger muscles, less lung power. We arrive at Scarlet much quicker than we left her. "Wow, you really live up to your motto," Kaylee says when we reach the end of the trail.

"My motto? What are you talking about?"

"The quicker picker upper. You practically ran down that hill." She laughs hysterically at my expense.

"Am I going to have to hear paper towel jokes for the rest of my life?" I ask. "And anyway, I'm the Brawny guy. Bounty is the quicker picker upper."

"Probably." She turns to get in the car and I grab a pine-cone off the ground and throw it at her, hitting her square in the back.

"Oh no you didn't," she says.

"Uh-huh."

She bends down, picks the pinecone up, and cocks her arm back. "Bring it," I say. She throws the pinecone and nails me in the forehead. I rub the spot where it hit. "Ow!"

Now we're both grabbing pinecones like maniacs and launching them at each other as fast as we can. I run after her and she squeals like when we were young and tries to get away, or maybe fakes trying to get away. I grab her around the waist and we both fall to the ground in a fit of laughter. My opportunity has arrived. It's time; I lean over her and kiss her, softly on the lips. They taste sweet just as I imagined. I pull back and look into her face, which has a strange expression.

"What was that?" she asks.

"I just thought—" I begin to say.

"You thought wrong," she says, standing up. "We should go."

"Kaylee, I'm sorry."

"It's fine, really. Let's just forget it. Come on, let's go."

We climb into the car, and Kaylee starts Scarlet up and revs her engine a couple times.

We stay quiet for a long time. Finally, Kaylee says, "I had a good time. Thanks for sharing it with me."

"'Thank you for sharing it with me'? What are you, a Hallmark card?" I joke, even though the weight of her rejection still crushes me.

"God, whatever," she says, smacking me. "I'm just trying to be nice, you dork. What's our next stop on your journey to self-fulfillment?" she asks, looking over to me, cute little smirk on her face.

"Trevor," I say.

"Ah, yes, Trevor. I was wondering when you'd get to him. When we were at the party and you told him you wanted to talk to him, I got curious. So, he's part of your little pilgrimage this weekend? Why?"

"I can't tell you."

"Of course you can't."

"I think he may just need someone to talk to," I say.

"What, do you think you're like Dr. Phil now or something?"

"Shut up and drive," I joke, though nothing seems funny to me right now.

"You know what, Austin?" Kaylee asks.

"What?"

"Sometimes you're a real pain in the ass."

chapter fourteen

Kaylee, used to the drill by now, puts her ear buds in place before I'm even out of the car. I walk toward the large west side home, noticing the plants and bushes along the pathway. Some of them are turning brown with the change of season. It's almost tragic, really, how much we take for granted the beauty that surrounds us every day. I mean, I must have walked by these plants thirty or forty times in the last few months, but this is the first time I've really looked at them. I bet they were amazing in full bloom, but now they've wilted, close to death, before I even realized they were here. It makes you think.

I arrive at the door and ring the bell. Suz answers; her face brightens when she sees me. I'm starting to think Kaylee's right. Maybe she does like me, something I've never bothered noticing before.

"Austin!" She wraps her arms around me and hugs me tightly. She holds on a little too long for my taste.

I push her away quickly, but gently; I didn't want Kaylee to see. I look back at the car. Kaylee's entire body is rockin' in rhythm to her iPod, her eyes closed. Not a care in the world. I turn back to Suz. "Hey, Trevor around?" I ask.

"Trevor? You haven't come to see me?" she asks. She bats her eyelashes as she moves in close, wrapping her arm in mine, which I immediately shake loose. I can't believe I've never noticed her advances before; they're so obvious to me now. She leans in right next to my ear and says, "You know, Austin, I feel a close connection to you, a kind of energy discharge whenever we're together. Do you feel it?"

Getting uncomfortable, I try to make a point, without really making a point. "All I'm really feeling right now is a little tired. Kaylee and I went hiking up at Mount Rainier earlier."

She backs off, hurt. She's sexy and all, but I just don't feel that way about her. "Oh" is all she says, eyes diverted toward the floor in what I can only imagine is utter embarrassment. I feel bad, hurting her like that, but I definitely don't want to lead her on.

"I really need to talk to Trevor," I say.

"Fine," she says pouting. "He's in his room."

"Thanks, Suz."

I head down the stairs to the Lair. That's what Trevor calls it, anyway. He's basically taken over the basement. It's the only space large enough for all his stuff, and I mean *stuff:* musical instruments, PlayStation, Xbox, and Wii. Why he needs all three gaming systems I'll never know. He also has a DVD player, movies, CDs, stereo, flat screen, laptop—he's spoiled. Both he and Suz are the result of divorced parents vying for, or rather buying, their kids' affection and attention.

When I enter Trevor's sanctuary, he's sitting on his bed, kicking back, reading a graphic novel. He greets me coolly. I'm not sure if he's angry with me for some reason or feels awkward about my visit. "What's up?" he says. He doesn't look up from his book.

"Can we talk?"

"About?"

"You."

"Me?" he says, finally looking up from his read. "What about me?"

"Well . . ." Thoughts rush through my head. Should I be doing this? Should I just mind my own business? Is this subject off-limits? Maybe I should just go. Will he even talk to me? I mean, we're friends, but more on a superficial level than anything else. He'll probably get pissed. My mouth doesn't listen to my head, as usual. "It seems like you've been going through some stuff lately."

"Stuff?" he asks.

"Yeah—um, we're good friends, right?"

"Sure."

"I just want you to know, you can talk to me. I'll take it to the grave, I swear," I say, crossing my heart with my index finger.

Trevor cringes at my words. "Why do you have to make jokes like that?"

"I don't know. To make things easier, I guess."

"For who?" he asks.

"For me, for you, for everyone."

"It doesn't make anything easier. I think it makes it worse. That's just my opinion, of course—take it or leave it."

"Sorry. Never thought of it that way," I say. Trevor always was oversensitive.

"So, what are we talking about here?"

Now I'm really worried that Trevor won't talk. "I was just saying that you seem to have a lot on your mind lately, and I wanted you to know that I'm here if you need someone to talk to."

"I don't have anything to talk about."

Crap. Failing. "Okay. I guess I'll go, then," I say.

"See ya," Trevor says. He goes back to his novel, but I see him watching me out of the corner of his eye.

"Yeah, later," I say, then get up to leave.

Before I reach the stairs he asks simply, "You know, don't you?"

"What?" I say, although transparently. Trevor eyes me. "Yeah, I know," I answer. I walk back toward him.

He folds his book, lays it on the bed. "How?"

"I saw you at an all-ages show at the Viaduct. Kaylee and I were there."

"Shit! Sometimes I don't think. I get careless. Did Kaylee see anything?" he asks nervously.

"No, I told her I got food poisoning and didn't feel good. We left before she saw anything."

Trevor lets out a heavy sigh. "Thanks, man. You're a true friend," he says, loosening up.

"Does your sister know? Or anyone else, for that matter?" I ask.

"No."

"Are you going to keep it that way?"

"For now, yeah. I'm afraid of how people will react. I don't want them to freak out or anything," Trevor says.

"How long? I mean, when did you know? When did it happen?" It feels like nothing's coming out right.

"My first happened maybe three years ago, but I guess I've felt it for longer than that. I struggled with the feelings, probably overcompensated with girls. Trying to make the feelings go away. Of course it didn't work. I experimented a little. Then I met Chris at a party a couple years ago. We've been together since. I've never felt like this before. Not even with Shelly Baker."

"Really?" I say. Shelly was Trevor's girlfriend in the eighth grade. They were always all over each other, everywhere—in the school hallways, at the dances, at the movie theater. Everywhere. They seemed attached at the lips. Thinking back, Trevor always had a girl by his side, sometimes more than one. I can see what he means about overcompensating.

"Yeah, I didn't even like her all that much. I guess it was just for show, because I was already having some feelings I didn't quite understand, you know. I almost felt like at times I was outside my own body, looking in, trying to figure out who the hell was in there. It was weird."

"I feel like that sometimes," I say.

He looks at me and says, "Yeah, I bet you do."

"So, what're you gonna do?"

"I don't know. Keep doing what I'm doing. Keep the secret, at least a while longer. Chris's friends and family don't know either. We're not ready for people to find out. I know Suz would be okay with it, and Kaylee, but my parents? Justin? I don't think so."

"Your secret is safe with me," I assure him. I go to leave, but before I do, I say, "I don't know for sure, but I think everyone who cares about you will understand and accept you for who you are. I know I do."

"I don't know, Austin. You really think so?"

"Yeah, I really do. I also think it's important for people to be who they are inside. Otherwise, it's like they're not being true to themselves, their true nature, and in the long run, the sneaking, the hiding . . . it'll make you crazy."

"You're probably right," Trevor says. "It's just not the right time. Not yet."

"I get that. Just know that there are people out there for you. I'll be here as long as I can."

"Thanks. I appreciate that." He approaches, gives me a quick hug, and pats my back like guys do.

"I have to go. I'll see you around, Trev."

"Hope so." I head back up the stairs, sneak out the door before Suz sees me, and get back into the car with Kaylee, who removes the buds from her ears.

"So?" she asks.

"It's all good."

"That's it? It's all good? You're really not going to tell me what's wrong with one of my best friends?"

"There's nothing wrong with him, Kaylee. He just needed

someone to talk to, one person he could confide in so he doesn't feel so alone."

"What? Is he gay or something?"

This catches me off-guard, but when I look at her, I realize she's joking. "Right. We're talking about Trevor here, the guy who used to get it on with Shelly Baker? Get serious."

"All right. Good enough," she says as we once again hit the road.

chapter fifteen

"Where next?" Kaylee asks.

"Bertram Brewster," I answer.

"Who?"

"He used to go to our school, left in third or fourth grade. Everyone called him Bertie," I answer.

"Nerdie Bertie?" she asks, her voice lacking any sympathy at all.

"Yeah."

"So what's his dilemma?"

"I hope he doesn't have one."

"Why? What's he to you?" she asks, now eyeing me suspiciously.

"I just need to talk to him."

"All right, Mr. Button Lip. Do you even know where to find him?"

"I think so," I reply, giving her the last address I could find.

Bertie Brewster was in my class from kindergarten until he left Skyline Elementary. With his small frame, glasses, high-waters, and lisp, he was a prime target for bullies. Unfortunately, for him, I was in my bullying prime at the time. I picked on all kinds of kids, but for some reason Bertie was my favorite. Maybe I was scared of what he was, afraid to be like that: small, weak, inferior. Now look at me. I'm pretty much there. The reasons don't matter anyway. What I did was wrong. I want to make it right.

We pull up to a house, but I'm not sure if you can even call it that. It's more of a shack, really, paint peeling, roof caving in, one window boarded up. If I blew on it, it would probably fall down. I double-check the address to make sure it's correct. I exit the car and head up to the dilapidated house. One of the address numbers on the front falls off when I knock on the door.

"Bertie! Get the door, God damn it!" At least I know I'm at the right house. The door opens moments later. I recognize him immediately: still small, but he's lost the glasses and is way more muscular.

"Yeah?" he says.

"Are you Bertie Brewster?" I ask, just for clarification.

He laughs. "No one but my mom ever calls me that anymore. It's Double B now. What do you want?"

"Well, Double B"—it sounds stupid coming from my lips—"my name's Austin. We used to go to school together. Do you remember me?"

"No," he answers, too quickly to have given it any real thought.

I breathe deeply. I was hoping he would recognize me so I wouldn't have to explain too much. I say, "My name is Austin Parker. We went to Skyline together."

"Nope, still doesn't ring a bell."

"I was kind of a bully. I used to pick on you."

Now he studies me carefully, every feature, every detail, up, down, round and round, side to side, until it becomes clear. Anger spreads across his face.

"I remember you. What the fuck do you want?" he says.

"I've just come to apologize. I want to say I'm sorry for the way I treated you back when we were kids."

"You should be sorry, asshole!" he yells. "You used to kick my ass every day. Kids made fun of me, and when I came home with a black eye or bloody nose, my parents couldn't even look at me. Do you know what it's like to disappoint your parents like that? How it feels to have them look at you and just shake their head, knowing they wished you weren't their kid? No, you probably don't, Mr. Perfect. You don't look so tough anymore. I bet I could kick your ass now—how would you like that?"

"I wouldn't like that at all. I just wanted to apologize. I don't want to fight," I say, trying to remain calm.

"Of course you don't want to fight. Look at you," he says, sizing me up again. "I've been working out. I'd wipe the floor with you." He puffs out his chest, beats it with closed fists like a gorilla. I almost expect him to belt out the Tarzan yell.

"Yeah, I can tell you've been working out," I say.

"Are you being smart with me? Huh?"

"No, really, I'm not, I mean it. I really just want to say I'm sorry. That's all." I back away slowly. Apparently, Bertie feels a latent hatred for me that has been awakened. Without warning, he punches me right in the face, tagging my nose and eye with one blow.

I hear Kaylee's door open. She flies out of the car screaming, "Stop!"

"Who's this, your bodyguard?" Bertie jokes, then gives me an uppercut to the chin, followed by a quick left hook to the mouth.

"Please," Kaylee begs. She grabs his arms, trying to pry them from me.

Bertie shakes her off and she tumbles to the ground. I hold back tears of frustration. I can't control anything. I have to watch Kaylee fall instead of protecting her. I'm useless and pathetic.

Kaylee gets back on her feet and jumps on his back just as he's grabbed my shoulder and is about to punch me again. "Stop! You don't understand. You could really hurt him," she cries.

Bertie finally looks at her. I mean, really looks at her. He immediately lets go, backs off as if I've become hot to the touch. I become lightheaded and fall to the ground. Kaylee bends over me as I bleed out my nose and mouth.

"Austin, are you okay?" she asks. Her tears spill onto me, mingle with my blood, drip down my face.

"I don't know. I think so," I choke out.

She turns on Bertie. "You fuck head! What's wrong with you?"

Bertie says, "He deserved it."

"We're even," I say weakly once I fully regain my voice. Kaylee helps me to my feet and to the car.

"You had some nerve coming here, asshole!" Bertie yells after us.

Just as she's about to get in the car, Kaylee flips Bertie off, then peels away. He chases after us shouting obscenities until he runs out of steam and gives up. When we're well away from Bertie's neighborhood, Kaylee stops by an AM/PM for ice. My entire face and body ache, the ice stings my forming wounds, but to lighten the moment I say through my hugely fat lip, "I know I've already plastered her with puke, but do you think Scarlet will mind if I get blood on her upholstery?"

Kaylee stays silent for a moment; she's taking long, decisive breaths. Suddenly, she unloads on me. "Goddamn it, Austin! What the hell are you doing! That guy could have killed you if he wanted to."

"Kaylee, we're all gonna die someday," I say.

"Yeah, we're all going to die someday. I didn't realize you wanted to do it today. Why don't I just drive you straight to the morgue and get it over with? And can you stop it with all your meditative 'Confucius Say' bullshit? What's the point, Austin? We all know you're a great guy. You don't have to prove it to anyone. Maybe you should just mind your own business. Let these people fix their own problems, live their own lives."

"But they're not, Kaylee. They're standing still while the world passes them by. It's not fair. They have a life to live. They have a future. I want for them what I can't have for myself."

"Austin, you can't take on the weight of the world. You can barely carry your own," she says, softer now.

"I know, but maybe I can make it a little bit lighter."

She expels a heavy breath, a deep sigh. She knows I'm right, knows this is something I need to do. She doesn't respond, and by saying nothing she agrees with me.

We drive a few miles in silence before Kaylee says, "Austin, I . . ." Then she pauses.

"What? What is it?"

"I, um . . ." She's struggling, whether it's to find the right words or any words at all, I don't know. "I worry." She sighs. She looks disappointed in herself, as if she wants to say something else but can't. "I don't like seeing you hurt. I, uh, care about you."

"Kaylee, can I tell you something?"

She completely ignores the question. "I mean, we're best friends. I just want you to be okay."

The *F* word again, the ultimate blowoff. "The stuff I'm doing, it's not just for them, you know. I have my own goals, my own needs."

"I get that, but no more of this stuff, okay? I can't bear to see you hurt. I lo—" She stops herself short again, thinks, then says, "I loathe it."

"You loathe it?"

"Yeah, I loathe seeing you hurt." I raise one eyebrow at her. "What?" she says.

"Is that really what you were going to say?" I'm ribbing her, I know, but it seems like she wants to say so much more.

"Yeah, sure. Why?"

"It just seems like a weird thing to say. 'I *loathe* when you get hurt'?"

She looks at me and giggles. "Shut up."

"Fine. I'll shut up." For the first time that weekend, our entire relationship in fact, I think maybe, just maybe, Kaylee might like me as more than just a friend.

chapter sixteen

I stare out the window admiring the Tacoma skyline as we head back to the more familiar parts of town. I pull out my camera and start filming video aimlessly as the sights speed by. We pass the Tacoma Dome. The once pride and joy of downtown Tacoma was host to now defunct Sabercats hockey, Tacoma Stars soccer, and even one season of the Seattle Supersonics. A bit rundown these days, but grand still, it now sees home and garden shows, art and craft fairs, concerts, and high school sporting events.

We take the 705 toward the north end, over the railroad tracks, past the museums, homes to history, art, and glass. I look over the Thea Foss waterway, new condos lining the west side, though nearly empty, having been built right before the recession. I look back over my shoulder at Mount Rainier. It seems like days instead of the few hours since Kaylee and I have been there.

I ask Kaylee to take the Stadium Way exit so I can absorb

mighty Stadium High School, the castle on the hill. We drive back down to the waterfront, where beyond the docks, restaurants, and the Puget Sound sit Federal Way, Browns Point, and Vashon Island.

We pass through a tunnel under the old smelter site, the aluminum smokehouse, once a landmark of Tacoma's waterfront, now just a fading memory, demolished just a few years back. That smelter was vital to many families in this area, including mine. It paid the bills for my grandfather on my dad's side. After it closed, he drank himself to death.

We enter Point Defiance Park and roll down the long, windy hill to Owen Beach. We get out of the car to walk across the beached logs and stick our feet in the icy water. Kaylee, Jake, and I used to come here a lot during the summers. We would just sit on the logs and talk, or walk down the beach and carve our names in the clay cliffs. Sometimes Jake would climb the steep hill leading up and away from the beach and try to ride his skateboard down. He crashed every time, even broke his arm once.

With daylight fading fast, we climb back into the Mustang. I have Kaylee drive me through Five Mile Drive, where we take in views of the Cascade and Olympic Mountains, the Narrows Bridges, and Gig Harbor. A sadness sets over me as we cruise past the now empty, rundown Never Never

Land, once a fantastical haven of life-size nursery rhyme and storybook characters. I brighten a little as we pass its neighbor, Fort Nisqually, an interactive living history museum that was once a Hudson's Bay Company outpost. This park holds many memories for me. They come rushing at me, full force, the picnics, the bike rides, the trips to the zoo. I begin to cry, to weep for them, these memories soon to be lost.

Kaylee pulls into a parking spot near the end of the park, next to the rose gardens and duck pond. She turns to me, puts a hand on my shoulder, and waits silently until she thinks I'm calm. "Are you okay?" she asks.

"I'm scared."

"Me too."

"I wish we could just hit the road and drive forever into nowhere." I look up at her, hot tears still stinging my eyes. "Until the end of time, just you and me."

"I wish we could too."

We sit in silence for a moment, just breathing, just being. "We could keep driving today. Did you have someplace else you wanted to go?" she asks, although I'm sure she already knows the answer.

"My dad's," I say.

Kaylee shifts the car into drive, as she's done so many times already this weekend, and heads toward the Narrows Bridge.

My dad moved out to Gig Harbor after he and my mother separated. They've been apart for five years now, though never brought themselves to divorce. Seems hopeful to me.

I've driven this bridge a million times, this old steel bridge built after the wind took the Galloping Gertie, the first bridge to span this section of Puget Sound. I respect its height and length. I know it's not as big or long as the Golden Gate and others, but it seems huge to me.

We cross, heading west toward Purdy, a drive of fifteen to twenty miles. We reach our exit; come to yet another bridge, this one diminutive and quaint, the kind you find in a small rural town. We pass a tiny grocery, ice cream parlor, and video store and continue across the spit through the windy, wooded roads leading to my dad's house.

We roll slowly, twisting and turning down the long unpaved drive, gravel grinding beneath the tires. Giant trees mark the edge of the driveway, stand as sentries guarding a hidden kingdom. Kaylee swerves to avoid a squirrel, almost smashing into one of the tall, impressive cedars.

"Smooth move, Ex-Lax," I say. She smacks my arm.

We come to a stop outside my father's little cabin. He lived in a travel trailer on the five-acre property, while building this place with his own hands. It's perfect for him, really; he always loved nature more than he ever loved people.

I climb the stairs to the homey porch, one you might see in a Norman Rockwell painting, complete with swing, muddy work boots, and my dad's bulldog, Dog. I asked my dad once why he named him Dog, and he said, "Because that's what he answers to. I say 'Come here, Dog,' and he comes. Seems silly to call him anything else." Reasoning I was unable to argue with.

I pat Dog on the head, approach the knotty pine door, and knock. No answer. I knock again just to make sure. Again, no answer. My dad's truck sits in front of the house, so I know he's home. I begin to hear a thunking sound coming from around the back of the house. I work my way back and find him chopping wood. I think he might be the only person left on the face of the earth that still chops wood. Everyone else just buys Duraflame. Yes, he's quite the outdoorsman—strong, rugged, wears flannel a lot, and always smells of Irish Spring. I've inherited his mouth, his height, and his outlook on life. He used to be clean-shaven, but since moving out to the woods, he's grown a mustache and beard. I hate the facial hair. I think I'll tell him.

"Hey, Dad," I say, approaching slowly. I don't want to startle him while he's holding an ax.

"Austin!" he greets me, throwing the ax dead center into a stump twenty feet to his right. He approaches me, arms outstretched, but stops short when he sees my face, recently beaten in by my old friend Bertie Brewster. "What happened to you?"

"I got into a bit of a fight."

"A bit of a fight? It looks like you got hit by a bus!"

"He was slightly smaller than a bus," I say.

My father looks at me with disappointment and concern. "You shouldn't be getting into fights," he says to me, as if I didn't know.

"It's not like I planned to get the shit beat out of me. Anyways, I had it coming," I say.

He puts an arm around my shoulders and leads me around to the front door. Upon seeing Kaylee relaxing in her car, he says, "What's Kaylee doing sitting out there in Glory? Does she want to come in?"

"No, I've asked her to stay in the car," I say. He lowers an eyebrow. "And the name is no longer Glory, it's Scarlet. Glory was like three names ago."

"How many times is she going to change the name? That poor car is going to have an identity crisis." We laugh.

"I guess as many as it takes to find the perfect one."

"So, to what do I owe the pleasure of your company?" Dad asks.

"I came here to talk to you," I answer.

"Okay, let's talk." He leads me into the cabin.

I do love this place, so close to the world just beyond the trees, yet so secluded, so quiet. The woodstove in the living room, set inside a hearth created out of nothing but river rock and pine timbers, already blazes with heat from the fire within. Above the stove hangs a picture of my parents and me during one of our hiking trips at Mount Rainier. Mowich Lake, if I remember right. The Comet Falls hike has nothing on the Mowich Lake hike. Switchbacks all the way up then down again to the lake. Once you enjoy your picnic and the view, you have to do it all over again to get back to your car. Takes the entire day and is quite painful. Well worth it, though.

It's rustic for sure, this cabin, almost looks as if it's been here one hundred years instead of four. I take a seat in the antique rocking chair next to the fire; my dad sits on the couch across from me.

"So, what is it you want to talk about?" Dad asks.

"Mom," I answer.

"Mom? Austin, there's nothing to talk about there. That chapter of my life is closed."

I said that two bad things happened in sixth grade: the first was Kaylee's dad dying, the second was my dad leaving.

"If it's a closed chapter, why haven't you two ever divorced?"

"It's just easier not to. Divorces can get sticky. You know—paperwork, custody, property division," he answers. "If your mom ever wanted to remarry, I would gladly sign the necessary papers."

"She doesn't want to get remarried," I say, getting irritated. "She still loves you."

"No, no, she doesn't. She made a choice, and she didn't choose me."

"I don't even know what happened. Why did you guys fall apart?"

"It's complicated."

"Why do people always say it's complicated when they don't want to talk about something?" I ask.

"Well, because it's easier," Dad replies.

"So, is that your answer for everything? To take the easy way out?" I ask.

"Sometimes things just aren't meant to be. We came from different backgrounds, different lifestyles. She couldn't get past our differences."

"Or maybe you couldn't," I say.

"You really want to know the truth?"

"That's why I'm here," I answer.

"It's not pretty."

"Sometimes life isn't pretty, Dad," I say.

"Yeah. It can be downright ugly, can't it?"

"Yep. It sure can."

"I loved your mother from the moment I met her. That pretty porcelain face, raven hair, deep green eyes. She was more than pretty; she was gorgeous. Still is. But she came from money, and her mom never liked me."

"Peggy," I say.

"Yeah, Peggy. I used to call her Piggy."

"Not nice, Dad," I say, but laugh in spite of myself.

"I know, but I can't stand that woman. We snuck around behind her back and finally eloped to Vegas. An Elvis impersonator married us."

"Seriously? Elvis?" I had no idea.

"Yes, seriously. Hang on a minute." He stands up, leaves the room, returns moments later, and hands me a photograph. Sure enough, the photo shows Mom, Dad, and Elvis under a white archway.

"Your mom has the rest of the pictures. You should ask to see them sometime."

"I will. Go on."

"What it comes down to is that your grandmother hated the idea of us together so much that she sabotaged us."

"How?"

"By interfering, sticking her nose in, pitting us against each other. But one night, after we fought, she plied her with liquor and pushed her into the arms of another man. Your mom cheated on me," he says.

"What!" I yell. "Mom had an affair?"

"I wouldn't exactly call it an affair," Dad continues. "More like a fling. And don't judge her. You can never judge someone unless you've walked in their shoes. Her mom was pressuring her, and I was alienating her. She cracked."

"What did you do?" I ask.

"I left," he says. I bring up my memories of the day he walked out the door. After the yelling and crashing and things had quieted, I slowly opened my bedroom door and went downstairs. My mom sat there on the couch, crying into her hands. I asked her what was wrong. She told me that she and Dad were having some trouble. That Dad left. I remember asking if he was coming back. She said she didn't know. He never did. After that it was every other weekend and alternating Wednesdays.

"You left right then and there?" I say, surprised at how dejected I suddenly feel.

"Austin, she cheated on me. In essence, she's the one who left the marriage, not me. Plus, she didn't try to stop me. I think if she had just said 'Stop' or 'Wait' or 'Don't go' as I walked out the door, I might have turned around. But she didn't, so I just kept walking."

I stand, pace the room a few times, let myself simmer, relax, chill. Deep breath in. "You know, she hasn't talked to her mother since then."

Dad seems surprised. "No, I didn't know that," he says.

"How could you? You've barely spoken to her," I say. "She still loves you, you know."

"She made her choice," he says.

"She needs you now. Soon she'll need you even more."

He looks at me thoughtfully, knowing I'm right. "We have our own lives now, Austin."

"No, you don't. You hide out here in the woods away from people, the world. She does nothing but work and garden. She has no life outside our home." He looks as if this information wounds him.

"You still love her, don't you?" I ask.

"Yes. I've always loved her, never stopped."

"Then fix this," I demand.

"How? How do I fix this after five years have passed?" he asks.

"Forgive her."

He sighs deeply as if just relieved of a heavy burden.

"I forgave her a long time ago, Austin, as soon as she apologized."

"She needs to hear it, from you. Go to her. Tell her."

"I don't know. It's been so long. I wouldn't even know what to say."

"Say, 'I love you; I forgive you.' It's easy."

"I'll think about it."

"I guess that's all I can ask."

We stand, walk to the door together; he hugs me tightly. "I love you," he chokes. He backs off, pats me on the arm, and brushes at his eyes to keep the tears from falling. I'm sure he wants me to leave before he cries.

"I love you too, Dad." I turn to go, but stop and turn back to him. "If you're going to do this, do it soon. Please?" He just nods.

"Thanks," I answer, beginning to tear up myself. "Oh, and one more thing?"

"What's that, son?"

"Lose the facial hair."

He gives me a surprised look and we both laugh.

I leave, shut the door behind me, slide back into Scarlet, and buckle up.

"Did that turn out the way you wanted it to, Austin?" Kaylee asks.

"I don't know. I hope so," I answer.

"Well, that's all you can do, right? Hope?" she says.

"Yes, I guess that's all any of us can do," I answer as we coast back down the long gravel driveway and back toward the highway.

chapter seventeen

"What's next on the agenda?" Kaylee asks as we reenter Highway 16 heading back toward Tacoma.

"Food," I answer.

"Thank God, I'm starved. Where are we going?"

"Frisko," I say.

"Mmmm, greasy goodness. I'm so there."

"There's one thing I want to do, though, before eating."

"Okay."

I have Kaylee take the Jackson Avenue exit off the new bridge, recently opened to control traffic flow and end the daily jams of the Gig Harbor commuters. I tell Kaylee to take the next two lefts. "Just park here," I say as soon as we turn the last corner.

We're sitting at the top of a hill overlooking the Sound, the bridges, and Gig Harbor. The homes in this area are new and big and must cost the bank for the view alone.

"What are we doing?" Kaylee asks.

"Just watch." The sun is close to setting, and on this clear September day, I'm sure it will be brilliant.

Kaylee cuts the engine, leans back, and says, "I love watching the sun go down. Have you ever been to the ocean and watched as it drops behind the horizon?"

"No."

"We should do that soon, maybe next weekend. I'll see if I can take the time off. We'll drive down Saturday, park on the beach, and watch the setting sun. Then we can get a cheap hotel room and come back Sunday morning."

"Sounds nice," I say, already imagining myself sitting on a blanket on the beach with Kaylee, wrapping my arms around her, keeping her warm, as the biggest star in the sky makes way for all the others. "But, no cheap hotel. We'll stay at a nice one, with a view. I'll pay."

"It's your dime."

We become quiet as the sun descends toward the other side of the globe. A sea of color bleeds into the sky, as if a rainbow has just spilled out over it. Yellows, oranges, pinks, and blues intermingle, fuse together, a surreal painting that only God himself could have created. As the sun plunges farther down below the horizon the colors dissolve into each other, until finally all is gray. Stars poke through the atmosphere, a prelude to the falling night.

chapter eighteen

We drive close to downtown, to the best burger joint in all of Tacoma. Frisko Freeze has been a landmark here for as long as I remember, though I know for a fact that my parents and grandparents frequented it as well. A classic drive-in, order at the window, eat it in your car kind of place. Everything but the roller skates.

We find a parking spot, and together approach the order window.

"Can I take your order?" It's Scott McPhee. From up close, he looks like shit. His once athletic body now sports a beer belly, his once shortly cropped hair now hangs down to his shoulders, matted and greasy. His clothes are filthy. He looks well beyond his twenty years by at least ten.

"Hey, Scott," I say.

"Hey, Austin, what's up?"

"Just getting some grub. How've you been?"

"Not bad. Surviving, you know."

"Yeah, I know."

Kaylee and I each order a cheeseburger and fries, banana shake.

We're quiet as we eat. I look over at Kaylee and she seems lost in thought, kind of mournful. She's staring out the windshield into nothing, eating almost mechanically. I want to ask her what she's thinking about but decide against it. Those thoughts are probably best left unspoken.

When I finish, I lie back in my seat, close my eyes, and just sit until I hear Kaylee slurping up the remains of her shake. I open my eyes back up. "You ready?" she asks. I remain quiet. Something, or rather someone, catches my eye. Scott McPhee is leaving work. He doesn't drive; he walks, head down, already lighting a cigarette. I watch as he strolls slowly down the street into the dark. His black pants and navy blue Frisko Freeze sweatshirt eventually blend in with the night and he turns invisible.

"I want to go see Scott."

"Why?"

"I want to know what happened to him," I answer.

"What happened to him? He's a drunk, that's what happened to him. What more do you need to know? He had his shit together too. What a waste," Kaylee says.

"Yeah, well, that's the point. What makes someone like Scott drown himself in alcohol?"

"Well, I guess we're going to find out, or you are, since

you won't tell me anything about your little visits," Kaylee says, driving down the street to Scott McPhee's apartment.

"Sorry, it's just, I mean, I've been talking to these people about really personal stuff. The secrets are theirs, not mine to tell."

We arrive at the apartment building Scott moved into after he graduated. From the looks of it, I would guess it's about ten floors. Kaylee drops me off out front, then leaves to find parking. A group of twenty-somethings smoke in the doorway. Inside, the lobby looks nice enough, but there's an unclean feel and smell that gives away what this place really is: a refuge for the outcasts, the aimless, and the hopeless. The couches and chairs in the lobby are covered in mysterious stains, and I can almost taste the film left behind by cigarette smoke residue. The place is in desperate need of a paint job, a steam clean, and more than likely pest control.

Approaching the elevators, I see one has a sign on it stating that it isn't working again, sorry for the inconvenience. I'm happy the other is in working order, as I'm not sure I could make it up six flights of steps to Scott's apartment. I hit the up button and wait. I enter the elevator, which smells like a combination of cigarette smoke, Lysol, and dog. I've only been to Scott's place one other time. He came to one of the soccer games my sophomore year. I wasn't playing; I was watching. We sat together, and he invited me and some of the team over to hang out.

Number 612. I approach the door and knock. Nothing. I knock again. It takes a while, and I'm about to give up, but finally I hear noise inside, a bump, a clatter, something crash to the floor, then a voice say, "Shit!"

Finally, the door opens and before seeing who it is Scott yells, "What do you want?"

"Hey, Scott, what's up?" I ask.

Scott squints his eyes as if his eyesight isn't so good, although I'm sure it's whatever he's drinking that's causing the blurring effects.

"Austin?" he says.

"Yeah," I answer.

"What the hell are you doing here?"

The question makes me feel awkward. "I thought maybe we could shoot the shit," I say.

"Now? I'm, uh, watching a movie right now. Can you come back another time?" he asks.

I peer inside; the TV isn't even on. I look at him gravely. "Scott, I'm not sure I'll be able to come back another time—ya know what I mean?"

He has a moment of clarity. "Oh, yeah, right, well, sure. Okay, come in, I guess." He steps back and allows me to enter.

The apartment is tiny and filthy. Clothes are flung every-where—doors, chairs, the floor. Dust has settled on tables and shelves. The place is scattered with cans and bottles of just about every kind of booze you can think of: beer, wine, tequila, whiskey, and a few things I don't recognize by sight. Strangely enough, there's not a food wrapper or box in sight, as if he survives on alcohol alone, or maybe he eats every meal at Frisko.

He clears a chair of clothing and other clutter and offers it to me. I cringe, but sit anyway. He heads to the fridge and grabs a beer. "You want anything, Austin?"

I decline, and Scott comes into the living room and sits on the couch. "So, what's up? What's going on?"

"That's what I've been wondering. What's been going on with you?"

"What's been going on? Look around you. This is pretty much what's been going on."

"I mean, what happened to you?" I ask.

"What? You don't think I'm living the life of a king?" The sarcasm doesn't suit him.

"No, I don't. You're so different. You used to be someone I admired, your persistence, your determination, your goals. I just wanted to know what made all that change for you."

"What changed, huh? Well, I'll tell you. Life kicked

me in the balls and I never got back up. That about sums it up."

"How exactly did life kick you in the balls? What happened?"

Scott lets out a weighted sigh. "Everything was going great. I got that full-ride scholarship from UP. Jeanie was going to go there with me." Jeanie was Scott's girlfriend, a cute little blond cheerleader. "She was so excited. God, some days I really miss her. She was so hot, and her rack! Man, she looked good on my arm." He drifts away momentarily. "The pressure was too much, the pressure to perform, to work, to get good grades. My parents harped on me nonstop. I lost it."

"Pressure? You lost it under pressure? No. No way. Not the Scott I know. You lived for pressure. You were made for pressure."

"Nope. It was too much."

"So then what?" I ask, not believing a word he's saying.

"Senior year I started drinking a lot. It got out of control. Jeanie broke up with me, my grades dropped, and I lost my scholarship. So here I am, living the big life in this crappy apartment, working at Frisko, barely getting by."

"I don't believe you," I say simply.

"You don't believe me? What's not to believe?" I can tell he's nervous, which tips me off that there's more to his story.

"Come on, Scott. Cut the shit. There's got to be more to it than that. I know you better than that. You were at your best under pressure."

His eyes shift; he stands up, paces. "There's nothing more, that's it," he says, now sweating, shaking.

"Yes, there is. What happened?"

"Nothing happened, Austin. Sometimes shit happens. That's all."

"Yeah, sometimes shit happens. I get that, but you were always above the shit in the world. Stop lying to me. Stop lying to yourself. I don't know why you're trying to make yourself believe the tale you're spinning, but it doesn't fly, not at all. Not with me."

"You don't want to know, believe me."

"Yes, I do. Come on, Scott. Level with me."

"No," he says harshly.

"This is bullshit and you know it."

"Drop it, Austin, seriously." He's agitated.

"No! Tell me what happened!" I'm yelling now. I'm not sure why.

"I mean it, Austin."

"Goddamn it Scott, what the fuck happened to you! Why'd you quit? You had it all. I wanted to be just like you."

Scott clasps his hands on top of his head. He paces, back and forth across the tiny living room. He sits down on the couch, buries his face in his hands, and cries, hard and heavy. I've never seen a grown man cry like this before. I never want to see it again. "Scott?" I approach, and lay what I hope is a comforting hand on his shoulder.

"You don't want to be like me. Oh, Austin, I'm sorry. I fucked up. I didn't know what to do," he cries. "I was scared."

"What to do about what?" I ask.

"I'm sorry, I'm so sorry." He continues to cry, tears, snot, and drool dripping down his face.

"Scott, talk to me. What happened?"

He takes a deep breath, sits up, and says, "I can't. You should go. I need you to go."

I don't know what to do. Do I stay and try and comfort him some more, or leave? I say, "Scott?"

"Please just go, Austin."

"Okay. I'll go. But I want you to know that you've meant a lot to me. You motivated me to do my best, and I hoped that maybe by seeing how you influenced me, that would help to motivate you."

"You can't help me, man. I'm cursed." He picks up his bottle and takes a swig.

I leave Scott sitting on the couch with a beer in his hand, regretful, tormented, and crying over some secret that changed the outcome of his life, a secret he's unwilling to share, one that may haunt him forever.

Kaylee is waiting for me at the curb when I exit the building. I slide into the car next to her.

"So, what happened?" she asks.

"I don't know. He broke down, but then he clammed up. I guess some people's demons are too strong to expel."

chapter nineteen

"Do you want to go home now?"

"No," I say. "Not yet."

"Okay, so what now?"

"*Superbad.*"

Kaylee sits up in her seat and exclaims, "Seriously? You're in the mood to watch *Superbad*?"

"Well, not really, but I need a laugh."

"I can't believe we're going to watch it again."

"What do you mean?" I ask, not believing she could even question my request.

"We've seen it a million times," she says.

"Come on. I am McLovin," I say, quoting the movie.

"Sounds like a sexy hamburger," Kaylee says. She's in. She rolls her eyes, and my heart skips a beat. Shifting Scarlet into drive, she heads to her house.

We pop some popcorn, even though we're both still full from dinner, but it's tradition. We settle into the couch and

Kaylee pushes Play on the DVD remote. I watch Kaylee more than I watch the movie. She laughs at the same scenes, the party, home ec class, the dick pics. The scene with the cops in the store is her favorite. She knows every line by heart, and nearly rolls on the floor when McLovin shows off his fake ID.

"Want me to take you home?" Kaylee asks once the movie ends.

"No, it's a nice night. You want to go for a walk?"

"Okay." We grab our coats and a blanket, and head out the door. We both know where we're going without saying a word. Mason Middle School. We love lying in the middle of the field on a clear night, looking up to the stars, imagining worlds beyond this one.

We find our spot, Kaylee lays the blanket on the cold turf and we lie down. My moment was not going to get any more perfect than this. It was time, my last chance; I have to fight my tongue, and fight my nerves, and tell Kaylee how I feel about her. Finally. Now.

I prop myself up on one arm, peer down into her beautiful face. "Kaylee," I say, relieved that my voice hasn't failed me yet again.

"Yeah?" she says, not having taken her eyes off the night sky.

"I need to tell you something," I say. My mouth is trying to procrastinate, but I fight to get the words out.

"What is it?" she says now returning my gaze.

I take a deep breath, close my eyes, and blurt it out. "I love you, Kaylee." My mouth won't stop now that it's begun. "I've always loved you, ever since the day we met on the playground. You've been on my mind constantly ever since, every day, every waking hour, and sometimes when I'm not awake." I reopen my eyes, one at a time, afraid of what her reaction might be.

It appears to be one of fear and shock. "No, Austin."

"You can't say no. I'm not asking for anything. I just wanted to tell you, before, well . . ." I say.

"You can't do this. Don't do this," she says, but she doesn't move, just lies there staring up at me.

"Why?"

"Because it's not fair. It's not fair to tell me this now. Jesus, Austin."

"I'm sorry. I just, well, I didn't want to leave without you knowing how I felt."

She sits up, grabs the back of my neck, pulls me close, and kisses me. Her lips are soft and gentle. They're salty, leftovers from the popcorn. "I love you too, you idiot. Why did you wait so long to tell me?" she asks.

"I don't know. At first I was afraid of messing up our friendship. I didn't want you to freak out and make you go away. I'd rather have you as my friend than not in my life at all. There were actually a couple times I tried to tell you, but after a battle with my stupid head and mouth, I lost. And then, up at the mountain, I thought—" I say.

"I'm sorry about that. I'm scared, Austin. I'm scared for you, about my feelings for you. I didn't want to love you if you were just going to end up leaving."

I lean in, kiss her again, longer. "I'm sorry I didn't tell you earlier. We would have had more time together," I say gazing into those deep blue eyes I'm crazy about.

"Me too," she says, and we kiss again, longer still. We lie back down on the blanket, still locked together, and stay that way, a moment I wish could be eternal.

She reaches under my shirt, rubs my back, pressing closer. I run my hand under her shirt as well, over her belly, under her bra. Her skin is warm, smooth, and soft. We undress each other, not caring that we're outside, in the middle of the football field, that it's September and the air is colder than it should be. It doesn't matter. Nothing matters right now except me and Kaylee. I take the edge of the blanket and throw it over us.

I keep kissing as my hand works its way back down her

body. She moans as I kiss parts of her I can't believe I'm touching. Her body tenses, she sighs, relaxes.

I'm nervous, an amateur, I fumble as I try to slide into her. She stops me. "You have protection, right?"

I smile, reach for my pants, pull out my wallet, and remove a condom.

"Oh my God, Austin. Tell me that's not the condom you've been carrying in your wallet since eighth grade," Kaylee says.

"No."

"But you've never, um . . ." she says.

"No, but I've changed it out, you know, every year or so." We both giggle. She pulls me down and again we kiss, and I stop fumbling.

"Oh my God, Kaylee. I can't believe we're here, like this."

"Me either."

"I love you."

"I love you too."

I've spent years anticipating this moment, but it seems only seconds in the moment itself. I'm embarrassed, but Kaylee doesn't seem to notice. I rest my head on her chest, and together we just breathe and fall asleep.

chapter twenty

When we wake it's late, and although I'd like to stay here with Kaylee as long as possible, I know I have to get home. There's one more person to talk to before bed. We walk back to Kaylee's house and she drives me home. I get to kiss her one more time before leaving. My mom waits for me in the living room.

"Austin, where the hell have you been? Do you know what time it is? And it's a school night," she says, as if I don't know.

"Sorry, Mom," I say.

She sees my battered face. "What in God's green earth happened to you?" *God's green earth,* a phrase spoken only by mothers, and they alone know its secret meaning. She runs over and inspects every scratch, every bruise, every wound. Her touch hurts.

"Mom," I say, pushing her hands away.

"Jesus, Austin, who did this to you?"

"An old friend," I answer trying to be funny.

"An old friend? I'd hate to see what your old enemies would do to you." I laugh, and upon seeing that I'm really not that damaged, she does as well.

"You should go to bed," she says.

"We need to talk."

"Tomorrow," she says.

"This is important."

She stares up into my face for a moment then says, "Hold on a minute." She gets up, heads to the kitchen, and comes back with a glass of red wine.

"The tone in your voice sounded as if I'd need this." I chuckle. "So talk."

"I just want to make sure you're okay," I say.

"Okay? Why wouldn't I be?" she asks.

"When I'm gone."

She quiets, breathes, sips. "I don't want to talk about that. Why do we have to talk about that?"

"I need to know that when the time comes, you'll let me go, move on. I don't want you to give up, to stop living, like Jake's mom."

"Move on? I'm your mother. You're my only child. How am I supposed to move on? You can't just move on from something like that. I don't want to talk about this."

We're silent for a moment, then I decide I just need to tell her. "I'm not doing another round of chemo."

Her eyes widen. At first I'm not sure what I see in them—surprise, yes, but then I think I see anger. No, that's not right. Fear, that's what it is. That fear quickly dissolves though, and she locates her sternest, most I'm-the-mom-I-make-the-decisions voice. "Yes. Yes you are. It's already scheduled."

I understand why she wants the chemo, but her reasons are selfish. I become frustrated, angry, I raise my voice, "No, I'm not. I don't want to." I begin to cry, and then sink to my knees in front of her and beg, "Please, Mom, let this be my decision. I'm dying. I'm never going to make it to eighteen. My body can't take any more treatment. It's tired. And what's it going to do for me? What did the doctor say? Maybe give me another three or four months."

"But those are three or four months of you still being here. With me. Don't you want to be here as long as you can?" She's crying with me now. I feel for her, but I have to make her understand how I feel.

"No, I don't, not like that. Those won't be comfortable, dignified months, no. They will be painful, horrible months spent in a hospital bed where I will be poked and prodded, and sick and miserable. It's not worth it to me for just another couple months of life. It won't be much of a life at all. I'm ready to go, I want to go, but I want to do it on my own terms, in my own house, in my own bed, my family and friends by my side. But I have to make sure you'll be okay."

She hugs me tightly. Her tears wet my cheeks, drip onto my shirt, sink in. Her lips right next to my ear, she whispers, "I won't be okay. I'm not ready. I'll never be ready. I don't want to let you go."

"It will be okay," I whisper back, for both of us, the tears now flowing freely, like rain.

She repeats the word *no* what seems like a million times.

"It's okay, Mom. It will be okay, I promise."

"You can't promise what you can't possibly know. Please don't leave me yet, Austin. I don't want to be alone."

"You won't be alone," I tell her.

She's listening to my words, but not to what I'm saying. She pulls my head in to her breast, kisses the top of my head. Now her tears stream onto my bare scalp, trickle down my cheek.

I pull away, grab her shoulders, look in her eyes. "You need to hear me." A confused expression spreads across her dampened face. She stays silent, so I continue. "Everything will be okay. You won't be alone."

"What do you mean? You're all I have in this world. Without you, it's only me."

"I've made sure," I tell her.

"Made sure?" she asks. "What do you mean, made sure?"

"I told Grandma to call you."

In a quiet voice she says, "Don't call her that. She's not your grandma."

"Yes, she is."

"I hate her."

"You can't. She's your mother. And whatever she did, I'm sure she's sorry for it. You should forgive her."

"It's a little too late for that now, don't you think?" she says.

"No, I don't think that. It's never too late for forgiveness." Mom lets out a deep, echoing sigh. "I think you'll be hearing from her soon. If she comes or calls, promise me you'll hear her out."

"Well, how can I turn down the request of a dying boy?" She says this quietly still, yet so sharp, it pierces my heart.

"Ouch," I say.

"I'm sorry, Austin."

"You may want to hold your apology."

"What? On second thought, hang on," she says. She

gulps down the remainder of her wine and goes back to the kitchen for another pour. She sits back down, takes another sip, and says, "Go on."

"I talked to Dad today."

"Jesus, Austin. Why?"

"Because you still love him, and you need him," I say.

"Austin, sometimes things are best left in the past. This is better for both of us."

"No, it's not. He loves you too, you know."

"He has a funny way of showing it."

"You hurt him. Bad."

She stands up, drops her glass. It tumbles through the air, as if in slow motion, and bounces silently off the carpet, wine splashing and seeping into the beige shag. I look down on it. It reminds me of blood.

"What did he tell you?" she says, her appearance calm, but her emotions I can tell are roiling right under the surface.

"He told me a lot, but I pushed him. Like you said, you can't turn down the request of a dying boy," I tell her, smiling.

"That's not funny," she says.

"It's not supposed to be, and it's okay. He forgave you a long time ago."

"Why didn't he ever tell me?"

"He thought you'd moved on."

"That's ridiculous. I was miserable, and he just up and left."

"You didn't stop him."

"He could have stopped himself," she cries.

"You broke his heart," I say.

"Yes, but he broke mine too."

"But now you can put them back together. You'll need each other. Soon."

She quiets, picks up the glass and refills it. "Yes, we will."

"He'll be by. I would bet tomorrow."

"Oh, you would, would you?"

"Yeah."

"Okay, genius, fine. I'll open my home, my mind, my heart, if it will make you happy."

"It will."

"I can't make any promises, though. It's been five years," she says.

"I'm not asking you to."

We sit quietly, she drinks her wine, I watch. Study. My dad's right. She's beautiful, with shiny black hair; of course, she's grayed a little the last couple years. Her eyes still shine like emeralds, and her skin is fair, like a doll's, but not pale. I've never noticed. I have her eyes; I used to have her hair.

"You want a snack?" she asks.

"It's late," I remind her.

"Yes, but I'm hungry. What do you want?"

"I'm not very hungry, but I'll stay up with you as long as you let me see your wedding pictures," I say.

"What?"

"Your wedding pictures. I want to see them. Dad showed me one with you guys and Elvis. I want to see the rest."

She smirks. After going over to the ottoman in front of the high-back chair, she lifts the lid. Funny, I guess I never really thought about what was in there. She reaches in, grabs the album, and brings it to me. She goes to the kitchen and comes back with a few crackers and slices of cheese.

"You have to have cheese and crackers with wine," she says. We sit silently. I flip through wedding pictures while she daintily eats her snack and finishes her wine. I watch her out of the corner of my eye. I think she needs this moment, when we just sit. It doesn't matter if we talk or stay quiet; she just wants to be with me not knowing how much time we have left together.

I hope she'll be okay, this woman who has been my anchor. I remember she used to cry a lot when I was a kid, out of joy or sadness I'll never know. She always made me feel so warm, so protected, so loved. I want that for her.

When the last crumb has been licked from her fingers

she says, "You should go to bed now. I don't want you skipping school tomorrow."

We rise and hug, and I head to the bathroom to brush my teeth.

I examine my cancer-ravaged body in the bathroom mirror. To me, I'm unrecognizable. My now naked scalp used to be covered with thick black curls. My skin, pale from hours of chemotherapy treatment, once looked healthy. This body, thin and weak, used to be strong and fit. I used to be normal, before the cancer. Now I *am* the cancer. It has coursed through my body, taking over, transforming me into some other being, someone alien.

I brush my teeth, my fatigue now catching up with me. I'm glad my body allowed me this weekend, kept going, didn't break down. I'm not sure if anything I did these last couple days made a difference. I wanted to reach out, let people know they still have a life to live, something I'll no longer have very soon.

And Kaylee. I'll die happy knowing she loves me. I wish I'd told her sooner. We could have had more time together, like tonight. I'll take advantage of the time we have left. Every second.

But first, I need to wrap a few things up, followed by sleep. I take the box I had shoved away up in my closet and place it on my desk. I take the DVD and concert poster that I purchased at the EMP and place them in the box. Removing the camera from my coat pocket, I also put it inside, on top of all my treasures. I sit down at my computer and begin to type.

"Dear Kaylee."

After I've said all the things I need to say, I fold the letter, slide it in an envelope, and place it on top of all my stuff, next to the camera. I put the lid back on but leave the box right where it is. Tomorrow I'll take it to Kaylee's and give it to her mother to keep until I'm gone.

I stare at the box and wonder how I got here. I remember when I found out about the cancer, I was in ninth grade. It didn't really hit me at first. It was like being in a nightmare and thinking at any moment you'll wake up and everything will be fine. It wasn't a nightmare, though, and I didn't wake up.

It was winter and I'd been sick. Since it was flu season, I thought nothing of it, just figured it would run its course. I hated being sick. Symptoms came and went, but eventually I'd been sick for so long on and off that my mom took me to the doctor.

After a physical and blood tests, the doctor called me back in for more tests. He said I had leukemia and sent us to an oncologist. More blood tests and bone marrow tests and he diagnosed me with acute myeloid leukemia.

I began chemotherapy treatment. Chemo sucked. I was in the hospital for nearly three weeks. I hated losing my hair, but the more I looked in the mirror, and the less people stared, the more I got used to it. The chemo made me tired, weak, sick. For months I dealt with it, and it seemed to be working, but then all of a sudden I relapsed. More tests, more drugs, and throw in some spinal taps and they found the cancer was growing again and it had reached my central nervous system. I was dying; there was no doubt in my mind.

My mom has scheduled me for another round of chemo, but I have resigned myself to the fact that very soon I will no longer be a part of this world. I will be gone and it will have to go on without me. I've accepted that there are so many things I haven't done, seen, and experienced.

And what about the rest of the world? What will things be like without me? I thought about all the people around me, the people I loved, the people I cared about. What would their lives be like when I was gone? That's when I started to worry. So many people I knew were barely even living their lives. Touched by addiction, violence, or loss, they had in a sense given up. I wanted to do something, to help, in whatever way I could. That's when I decided to take my journey.

I slip into my pajamas and lie in bed, resting, relaxing, letting my mind drift off. I know my time is short. I'm scared, but I try to hide it. I need to be strong for my family, my friends, especially my mom and Kaylee, but I know it's coming. I can feel it.

the end . . .

chapter twenty-one

I don't get to take that trip to the ocean Kaylee and I had talked about, because without any kind of treatment, the cancer moves quickly and I'm too sick. Instead she comes over and I make her describe in detail what it would have been like, from the car ride, to the weather, to the colors in the sky as the sun is swallowed by the horizon.

As the cancer progresses, so does the pain. Morphine helps. The doctor has given me up to six months, but within weeks I'm bedridden, too weak to move much at all. Hospice comes in, sets me up with a hospital bed and oxygen tank. They care for me when my mom needs a break: rub my back, bathe me, help me use the toilet.

The days are long and lonely, with everyone either at work or school. I sleep, listen to music, watch TV, and think about school, wishing I could be there. It's funny, actually wishing to be at school. How many times, sitting there in chemistry or history, did I wish I were somewhere else? Anywhere else.

I was wrong about my dad. He didn't call the next day. He didn't have to. My mom called him as soon as I went to bed that night. He moved in the next morning. He sleeps in the guest room for now, but it's temporary I'm sure. I think once I'm gone, they'll sell this place and my mom will move in with him, into his cabin in the woods. The memories from this house will be too much for her. Death will linger here.

Visitors come and go, family and friends, neighbors and teachers. Some mean more to me than others. Mrs. Briggs, Jake's mom, visits only once. The visit is short but significant. She looks better than when I saw her last. There's still sadness about her, but she's livelier, seems happier, halfway back to the Mrs. Briggs I used to know.

She brings books, pictures, CDs, and photos all having belonged to Jake, things she thinks will hold meaning for me. They do. She wants me to enjoy them while I'm still here. She tells me to pass them to Kaylee or Justin, or whoever I see fit when I'm done. I promise her I will. I can tell the visit is difficult for her. She shakes, fights tears, paces. Watching me die is like losing Jake all over again.

Trevor and Suz visit together a few times. They bring CDs to listen to, and Trevor reads graphic novels to me. Suz always cries. Trevor doesn't let his secret out before my death, and I take it to the grave as promised. Once he left Suz behind and brought Chris, his boyfriend, instead. He seems nice.

Justin and Steph come to visit together, though they have broken up yet again. They have a crappy relationship. Maybe they should just break up for good. Steph cries while she's here. Justin says he'll think of me whenever he's on the soccer field.

Mrs. Davis, Kaylee's mom, and her sisters, Jordanne and Maddie, visit a few times. Mrs. Davis brings me magazines and comic books and always sits quietly holding my hand.

Maddie sits in the corner trying desperately not to cry, but I know the tears are there, just beyond her pretty blue eyes, eyes not so unlike her sister's. She doesn't speak. I'm sure she's afraid that if she opens her mouth, the tears will flow. She reminds me of her mother, after her dad's death. She's trying to be strong for me. She doesn't have to; I can be strong enough for the both of us.

Other than the hellos and goodbyes, Jordanne is the only one who speaks when the three of them visit, talking endlessly about school. She sings to me Disney songs, "You've Got a Friend in Me" mostly. They've told her I'm sick, but not that I'm dying. Often she asks how long I'm going to be sick. I hope my death is not too hard for her.

Yelling echoes throughout the house the first time Peggy

comes to visit me. Not tended to, the wounds are still raw, like an unbandaged cut. Only a few words drift from the living room, up the stairs, and into my bedroom. I catch a few of them, the most memorable being "busybody," "bitch," and "why."

After a while the voices calm, then quiet. It's a long time before Peggy shows up to my room, and when she finally does, she's crying. I'm sure the tears are a mixture of joy and sadness. For the sake of my family, I hope I go quickly. I don't like to see them hurting.

Allie visits a couple times a week. She's letting her hair go back to its natural color, and it looks terrible, with light blond roots and jet black ends. I'm sure it will look fine when it's all grown out. When she comes, she's sober, something I haven't seen in a while. We talk about school, movies, and music. Stupid meaningless stuff. I think she likes to pretend that I'm fine and will be back at school in a day, a week, maybe a month, instead of dead. She kisses me on the fore-head every time she leaves.

Kaylee visits every afternoon. She's taken a leave of ab-sence from work in order to spend every moment outside of school or sleep by my side. We kiss, she reads to me, we hold hands, she lies on my bed next to me, we listen to music together, watch movies. I get to watch *Superbad* with her two more times before death comes for me. She doesn't laugh as she usually does when we watch it.

She cries when she thinks I'm not looking. I tell her not to be sad, to do it for me. I know I'm manipulating her, but I have to hear her say she'll be okay before I go. She says she will. I never let her leave without telling her how much I love her, which has become difficult because as the cancer worsens, I never know if it will be the last time I see her.

The disease has completely taken over my body to the point that I can't move at all. The hospice nurse raises my morphine dosage. My mother thinks the morphine is making me incoherent, killing me. The nurse explains that it's not the morphine but the cancer. My body is shutting down. The morphine makes it as painless as possible, that's all. She stands in the hallway outside my door with my parents and tells them it won't be long now. She thinks I can't hear, but I do, and it doesn't bother me. I didn't lie when I told my mom I was ready.

Life is subjective as far as memories are concerned. I mean, what pieces of your own life do you really remember? Some good times, some bad times definitely, but mostly you remember those times that really stand out, those times that define who you are as an individual. Now's the time my life flashes before me—flickering recollections, vacations, holidays, friendships, the moments that made a difference. Mostly I remember that weekend with Kaylee.

It's almost time to go now. Although I can't see her anymore, I feel my mom's hand holding mine. She stays true to her word and lets me know that it's okay to let go, to move on, to follow the light. She tells me that they'll be okay, she and Dad. They're at my bedside when I die. I feel their constant presence.

When death finally comes, it brings relief, and I hope not just for me, but also for everyone around me. It's time for them to close the Austin chapter of their lives, put it on a shelf, bring it out only when needed, when they want to remember. That's what I want. That's what I worked for that weekend that feels like so long ago but wasn't. I want them to feel peace, joy, and happiness. I want for them what I no longer have myself. Life.

The End

memories . . .

EPILOGUE

Kaylee is in bed, still sleeping when the call comes. It's early, not quite six o'clock, when her mother enters her room. She's holding a shoebox, the box that Austin had given her to pass to Kaylee upon his death. She sits on the edge of Kaylee's bed, tears glistening red, reflecting the light of the digital alarm clock. She sets the box down at Kaylee's feet, and waits. She waits until the right words come to her. How do you tell your daughter that her best friend, the love of her life, is dead? Yes, they were expecting it, but that never makes it any easier, does it?

This is the third time she's had to tell her daughter someone close to her, someone she loves, has died. It won't be easy, it never is. Kaylee was young when her father died, old enough to understand it but maybe not old enough for that loss to fully impact her emotions. Jake's death was difficult. To lose a friend like that, someone you spent just about every waking hour with, someone so full of vitality and life, someone whose death never received justice—it was difficult for her. But this one, this would be the hardest. To lose the person who's like the sun to you, warm and bright and essential to your survival, the person who makes your heart flutter like a million butterfly wings and your pulse race like wild horses, that one person you would give the sky, the sea, your very breath if you could. It's resonant. And her mother knows all too well what it's like to hear that kind of news. She knows it will be the worst pain Kaylee will ever suffer. It will crush her very being, suffocate her. It will leave her hollow.

She doesn't want to do it, but she knows she has to. Putting it off won't make it go away. She puts a hand on Kaylee's shoulder, gives a gentle shake, waits for her to stir.

Kaylee wakes slowly. She hasn't slept much as of late, having gone to Austin's most days before school, and then staying late into the evening afterward. She blinks, stretches, eyes open. "Mom!" she shouts, startled to find her there. She reads her face and knows immediately. "No," she cries. Her mom gathers her in her arms. "No!" she screams, tears streaming down her face. Her mom lets her weep, to let it out as long as she needs to. Kaylee cries herself back to sleep. Mrs. Davis lays her back down gently and leaves her to her dreams.

Waking, Kaylee sits up, sees the box at the foot of her bed. She grabs it, reads the front. It says "To my beautiful Kaylee, from Austin." Tears pour from her eyes. She puts the box back where she found it, stares at it. She's not ready. She showers, dresses, picks up the box again, puts it back down, eats breakfast, brushes her teeth and hair, cries. She picks up the box, needs some air. Cradling the box under her arm, she runs down the stairs, grabs her keys and purse, and heads out the door.

Scarlet roars to life, but Kaylee keeps her still. The name seems dumb to her now. It's just a color, or the protagonist from an old book, or a murder suspect from a board game. Scarlet is not the name for a car. Apple. That's what he wanted. It seemed fitting now. She won't change the name again.

Driving without purpose, Kaylee finds that Apple is guiding her to some of the places she and Austin had visited just weeks prior: Old Town, the waterfront, Point Defiance. She stops at Owen Beach, gets out, walks along the shoreline. She welcomes the cold, stinging wind, imagining it's Austin's spirit walking with her, enveloping her in its, his, chilly embrace.

Kaylee sits on a rock at the far end of the beach near the clay cliffs and watches as the waves crash into the shore. Bringing her knees to her chin, she wraps her arms around herself and weeps once again. When the tears have run their course, she rises, grabs a stick from the beach, approaches the cliffs, and carves "Kaylee Loves Austin" into the cold wet clay. She wonders how long their names will last, and keeps her eyes on them as she walks back down the beach, afraid they will fade as soon as she turns away. As she climbs into her car, her eyes sting, but she puts the Mustang in gear and rolls through the curving wooded roads that lead to the park exit.

Kaylee finds herself driving past Austin's house on her way home. On the outside, everything appears so still, so quiet. She's sure it's different inside, screaming, crying, anguish. The same anguish she feels coursing through her body straight to her core. She wants to stop, but the pain is still so fresh, not just for her, but for Austin's parents. Time. They need time not to have to be strong, time to grieve with abandon.

Continuing home, she realizes she's ready. She immediately climbs the stairs to her room, sits on the floor, and opens the box.

It's stuffed full of memories. Some items she immediately recognizes, some she's never seen before. On top of all that sits an envelope. She opens it and pulls out a letter. She begins to read.

Dear Kaylee,

If you are reading this letter, that must mean I'm not around anymore. I'm so sorry we didn't have more time together. Nine years just didn't seem like enough, did it? I would have liked to date you, marry you someday, have a family, grow old together.

I would have liked to be with you forever, but God had other plans for me. Know that I have loved you always, and will continue to love you even in death.

Not to kill the moment, but I have to get down to business. First things first: my funeral. I've left my plans with my parents, but you have to get them to follow them. They'll undoubtedly try to hold some lame cryfest at some stuffy church I've never stepped foot in. That's not what I want. I want a celebration. I want people talking, joking, and laughing. I don't want anyone mourning me.

I want you to give my eulogy. I know it will be hard, because I'm sure you're hurting right now. I know I would be if the shoe was on the other foot. But no one knows me better than you, Kaylee. I don't care what you say, a little, a lot, crying, smiling, laughing, but I want my memory honored in your words, with your voice.

My next order of business is music. My mom will try to play some depressing religious hymns. Don't let her. No dirges. There's one song you must play. Other than that, play what you want. The CD is in the box on top—it's black with the moon on the cover. Track number four is the one I want you to play. That song means a lot to me. Listen to it. You'll understand.

Please DO NOT wear black. Wear pink or green or purple or any other color of the rainbow. Actually, wear blue. You look beautiful in blue. It brings out your eyes. But no black. This is not a sad day. I'm no longer sick, no longer in pain. I'm okay now. I died happy—mostly because of you. :)

And for shit's sake, do not let my parents stick me in a box in the ground. Yuck! I don't want any damn worms crawling through me, eating my flesh. Sorry, that's a bit sick, isn't it? I want my body cremated. They can put a place marker wherever they want, but do NOT let them place me in the cold hard earth. Scatter my ashes on Mount Rainier, up by Comet Falls. You'll have to be sneaky about it, because it's frowned upon. I think it might actually be illegal, but that never stopped you before, right? Kidding. Please make this happen. I want to be up there among the trees and flowers, and fresh air, with the water flowing nearby. I want to be a part of that nature I loved, that nature my parents shared with me, and I shared with you.

Now that that's taken care of, back to the box. This box contains items that were important to me, us, our life together. Share them, keep them to yourself, use them as you wish. Many are pictures of our times together, alone, with our friends, at school, during the holidays, on our journeys. There's one of you in there that I LOVE. Jake took it. We're at Owen Beach, your hair is blowing in the wind, and you're looking out over the water. You looked like you were dreaming of some faraway place. I remember wishing I were there with you, inside your head, seeing what you were seeing. Anyway, you were looking out over the water, and there I am just beyond you, staring, gazing really, taking in the beauty and wonder that is you.

If you had seen that picture, you would have known I loved you. Jake did. He knew right away. That asshole held it over my head forever. Made me lend him money all the time or else he'd show you that picture. What a jerk, huh? His mom gave me the picture, and now I'm giving it to you. It's near the top of the box, so you shouldn't have trouble finding it.

There are a couple books in there, my favorites. Catcher in the Rye, Fahrenheit 451, To Kill a Mockingbird, Wuthering Heights, Lord of the Flies. *I know you've probably already read them all, but if you happen to read them again, I hope you'll think of me.*

I left you all of my indie CDs. My mom will give them to you later. I've placed my favorites in the box. I know you don't like indie now, but I think the more you listen, the more you'll appreciate it. Pay careful attention to the words, the meaning behind them. Try it for me. I mean, you can't live on hip-hop and pop alone. That's just wrong.

My poetry book's also in there. So many of the poems I've written have been inspired by you, or were written for you, so I think it's only right that you should be the one to have it. Share it if you must, but remember how guarded I was about my writ-

ing. Many of the words in that book were meant for you. I wouldn't mind if you kept it that way, a secret, close to your heart.

The last item is my beloved Cyber-shot. I've not yet downloaded the pictures or video from our journey together, so they're all still in there. Enjoy. I did. It was a beautiful weekend. I would have never forgotten it, and I thank you for that.

All of these items that once belonged to me now belong to you, along with your memories. I don't want you to mourn me, but I wouldn't mind if you thought about me from time to time maybe next time you eat at Frisko, or maybe while you're just driving aimlessly, letting Scarlet guide your way (you should really change her name to Apple by the way), or when you look up toward the night sky. Move on, live your life, Kaylee, but please, never forget me.

Eternally yours, Austin

Kaylee finds the photo, the one Austin spoke of, quickly. He was right; it was obvious. She should have known, even before he told her. She'd felt his gaze on her more than once. She figured she was just being delusional. Maybe she's the one who should have spoken up sooner.

She leafs through the rest of the photos, laughing and crying as she consumes memory after memory made timeless and everlasting through the lens of Austin's camera.

She pulls out the books, one by one, studying their covers. She's read them all but knows she will read them again, because they were his. She tries to decide which she should read first, and settles on the Brontë, the only romance in the bunch.

It's time to look through the CDs. She immediately opens the one he described in his letter. She puts it in her CD player, presses Play, and almost immediately realizes why Austin loved this music so much. So much feeling, so much meaning, it cries out for attention. She'll never listen to music the same way again.

His poetry book, the little spiral notebook with all his inner thoughts and feelings, comes out next. She opens to a random page and begins to read the poem within its lines.

"Stolen Heart"

She shimmers, not unlike the stars.
Gleaming, glimmering, glowing.

She sways, like the ocean waves.
Surging, rushing, rolling.

She's bright, she is the sun.
Blinding, dazzling, stunning.

She floats, quite like the birds.
Climbing, fluttering, soaring.

She's stolen my heart, with her it stays.
Clasping, keeping, owning.

My love is hers and hers is mine.
Falling, twisting, holding.

Crying, she closes the book, holds it to her heart, then lays it down gently on the floor.

Last, she picks up the camera, passes it from hand to hand, turns it, and examines it as if it's a foreign object. Leaning back on her bed, she pushes the power button and scans through the pictures one by one, slowly as to not miss a single detail. She plays each video, over and over, just to see Austin alive and animated again, to hear his voice. She puts everything back into the box, goes to her desk, sits in front of her computer, and sets the box down next to her. Placing her fingers on the keyboard, she begins typing the eulogy of Austin James Parker.

Acknowledgments

So many people to thank—where does one start? I suppose it's only right to thank my mother-in-law, Judy, first. It was after her death that I sat down and wrote my first novel. Through her death I also gained the experience needed to write this story. I've missed her these last nine years.

Next, I need to thank all of those who read the novel and gave me feedback, whether it was blanket ideas or full-on line edits. That would be Jarucia Jaycox Nirula, Debbie Mercer (and Mike Sullivan for bringing us together), Michelle Humphrey, Jay Simons, Chris Brown, Kristen Kendle, Kathy Vinyard, and my niece Lily Galagan, who gave me that teen perspective I so desperately needed.

There are three special friends I have to thank: Gae Polisner, who also read *Never Eighteen* in its early stages and gave me priceless advice; Jeff Fielder, who gave me the name of my agent, Irene Kraas, when I was just about to give up; and Tracy Walshaw, who motivates and inspires. The friendship these three have given me these last few years has been invaluable, and there are many days I'm not sure I would have made it through without them. They make me laugh, think, and work to be a better writer and a better person.

I need to thank my amazing agent, Irene Kraas, who had

faith in a little teen novel, at that time titled "Mending Fences." She took me in when I was about to give up, and remarkably sold my novel in two weeks.

To Julia Richardson, my wonderful editor who puts up with my endless questions, and has made revisions and copyedits fairly pain-free.

To my family, my parents, Guelda and John Messina, who never lost faith in me through the years, though I know I must have caused them some grief. To my brother and fellow writer, John Messina, who has read my stuff and given me positive reinforcement. To my sister Maribeth, who keeps me sane at my day job. To my sister Dana, who didn't kill me when I was little (and helped with my first-pass pages).

To Rusty Bostic, without whom this story would never have been written. He has been my idea man and best friend since the onset of my writing career.

Last, I thank my daughters, Mary and Rachel, for being my motivation to turn this hobby into a profession, and inspiring me every day (even the days when they drive me nuts).

Never Eighteen Playlist

Music often inspires my writing. You may have noticed songs and music mentioned throughout *Never Eighteen*. I wanted to use lyrics from some of the songs below, but because permissions are hard to get, I could not. Other songs on the list just inspire the spirit of the book. Here's the *Never Eighteen* playlist:

"I Will Follow You into the Dark" by Death Cab for Cutie
"New Slang" by the Shins
"Bulls on Parade" by Rage Against the Machine
"Soul Meets Body" by Death Cab for Cutie
"All Possibilities" by Badly Drawn Boy
"Where the Moss Slowly Grows" by Tiger Army
"Sometime Around Midnight" by the Airborne Toxic Event
"Chasing Cars" by Snow Patrol
"Fix You" by Coldplay
"Brick" by Ben Folds Five
"Red Right Ankle" by the Decemberists
"How We Operate" by Gomez
"Love's Labour's Lost" by the Less Deceived
"Weighty Ghost" by Wintersleep